D0171069

Jemima, Grandma
and the Great Lost Zone

by the same author

ELLIS AND THE HUMMICK
THE ABRADIZIL

JEMIMA, GRANDMA AND THE GREAT LOST ZONE

Andrew Gibson

illustrated by Chris Riddell

faber and faber
LONDON · BOSTON

First published in 1991
by Faber and Faber Limited
3 Queen Square London WCIN 3AU

Photoset by Parker Typesetting Service, Leicester
Printed in Great Britain by Clays Ltd, St Ives plc

A CIP record for this book
is available from the British Library

ISBN 0 571 16455 2

To Jos and Dan, of course,
and to Pete and Jill, as well

One

'Are you reading me?'

Jemima yawned.

'I don't believe you are paying the slightest attention, Jemima.'

It was Beatty. Beatty was one of the computers. His real name wasn't Beatty at all. It was BT 758. But Jemima always called him Beatty. Jemima stared grumpily at Beatty's screen. It was her homework. Astrophysics again.

'I'm bored,' said Jemima.

'To be bored,' said Beatty, 'is to be in error. One should persevere. Perseverance is a sign of greatness of soul.'

'Greatness of *soul*?'

'Yes.'

'You wouldn't know the first thing about it, Beatty,' said Jemima. 'You're a computer.'

'Today's computers,' said Beatty, 'have been endowed with awesomely extensive reservoirs of knowledge.'

'Well programmed, you mean,' said Jemima.

'A remark,' said Beatty, 'that was merely intended to wound.'

'You were programmed to say that, too,' said Jemima.

'Are you sure?' said Beatty. 'Is it not possible, after all, that I am a computer that has actually begun to THINK FOR ITSELF?'

Jemima laughed. 'No,' she said, 'it's not. You tried the same trick last week. It didn't work then, either.'

'You are an unbeliever,' said Beatty.

'No,' said Jemima, 'I just know you.'

'Let us recommence,' said Beatty. 'If the light particle in question travels in the . . .'

'I don't think I want to,' said Jemima.

'Further resistance will have unfortunate consequences,' said Beatty. 'Let me repeat: one should persevere.'

'I know what's coming next,' said Jemima. 'Rules, regulations, duties and punishments.'

'I shall report you to your father. This is your first ultimatum.'

'I'm so bored I could scream.'

'Second ultimatum now in force.'

'I think I'll go and see Grandma.'

'You would be ill advised to do so. This is your third and last ultimatum. Let me remind you of the rules, regulations, duties and punishments . . .'

'I'm going,' said Jemima. And she went.

*

I expect you're wanting some facts.

It was the year 2791. Jemima was on the *Andromeda*, deep in outer space. The *Andromeda* was a ship in Galaxy Patrol, and Jemima's parents were the commanders of the *Andromeda*. Wherever they went, Jemima went too. So did Grandma. Not without complaints.

Grandma was small and wizened. She had lively eyes and a funny, crackly voice. Jemima liked her better than anyone else at all.

Now, Jemima found Grandma in a rest room. Grandma was reading a book.

'Grandma,' said Jemima, 'I'm *bored*.'

'Perfectly understandable, dear,' said Grandma, still reading.

'What do you mean?' said Jemima.

'Look where we are,' said Grandma, waving a hand.

Jemima looked.

'Space,' said Grandma. '*Not on Planet Earth*,' she hissed.

Not long ago, Jemima's mother and father had decided that Grandma was too old to live alone on Planet Earth any more. She would have to live in space with them, they said. Grandma refused. They insisted. Grandma yelled. Father stayed firm. So there Grandma was, in outer space, grumbling. She often grumbled about outer space. Secretly, of course, she rather enjoyed her new life. But she never admitted it – least of all to Jemima.

'Well, I think Planet Earth is boring,' said Jemima. 'Crowds, *everywhere*. Robots and machines. False voices and tinkly tunes. And the people are so unpleasant, too.'

'You liked the Sahara Garden,' said Grandma, 'the one in North Africa.'

'No I didn't.'

'The Antarctic Fun Park. You liked that, too.'

'Huh. All those people whizzing about under the ice-cap in their little submarines, thinking they were being brave. It's only old folks who want to stay on Planet Earth, like you.'

'Sometimes, my dear,' said Grandma, mildly, 'you really can be quite offensive.'

'Well, tell me what else there is to like there.'

'The simple things. Sea breezes, for instance, at dusk.'

'Huh,' said Jemima. 'They're all poisoned. And

anyway, there are sea breezes all over the Universe. What about Alpha Nine-Four?'

'Ahah,' said Grandma, 'but they were *tempests*. Do you recall my little felt hat? They virtually blew it into orbit, you know.'

'They nearly blew you into orbit, too,' said Jemima. They giggled for a while. 'It never suited you in any case,' said Jemima, at last. 'Lots of planets have seas and lots of the seas have breezes, too. You just sit in the spaceship and read, and so you never notice.'

'And you,' said Grandma, 'are making the Universe up as you go along.'

A shape appeared at the door. It was Birmingham. Birmingham was a sort of computer on wheels. He looked like a very large egg on a rather small trolley. He had two little arms, two red eyes, and an aerial on top.

'Anyone for chess?' he said.

'No,' said Jemima.

No one ever wanted to play chess with Birmingham. The sad fact about Birmingham was that he malfunctioned. With Birmingham, chess soon turned into a different game. Ludo, for instance, or draughts. Even, on occasions, darts. In fact, Birmingham wasn't really any good at anything at all. Jemima and Grandma loved him.

'In that case,' said Birmingham, 'perhaps we could have an argument. I like arguments.'

Grandma smiled uneasily.

'Arguments,' she said, 'can sometimes be dangerous things.'

Jemima was more direct. 'The last time we had an argument, Birmingham, you started rattling like mad.'

'We had to take all your fuses out,' said Grandma, nodding her head.

'Oh dear,' said Birmingham. 'How very distressing for you. I'm afraid I don't remember the first thing about it.'

'I know,' said Jemima. 'Your memory bank doesn't work properly, you see.'

'Birmingham,' said Grandma, affectionately, 'you are a complete disaster.'

All at once, there was a hooting sound.

'JEMIMA!'

Jemima looked up. It was her father on the telescreen, with his sleek dark hair and his shiny blue suit. The face was tanned and calm. The voice was cool and brisk.

'They've been doctoring the wrinkles again,' said Grandma, dispassionately.

'Where are you, Jemima?' said the face.

'Rest Room 5, Father.' Jemima pressed a button next to the screen.

'Ah yes. I can see you now. Jemima, BT 758 informs me that you have not done your astrophysics homework yet. I presume this is true?'

'Yes, Father.'

'How very tiresome,' said the face. 'You have disarranged your schedule for the whole day. I'm afraid I shall have to see you for a moment. To emphasize certain points. In the main control room, please.'

The face vanished. Jemima scowled. Grandma scowled, too, in sympathy.

'Grandma,' said Jemima, 'I'm *bored*. Not just any old bored. Really, truly bored. FEARFULLY bored. So bored I could . . .'

'We'd better go, dear,' said Grandma, 'before you do,' and she hurried off.

*

The control room was a huge silver cube of metal, plastic and glass. It was full of crew, the way it always was: men and women, black, yellow, brown and white. They were all busily gazing at keyboards and screens. Everywhere you looked there were buzzers, panels of buttons, lights. Jemima's mother sat at one end of the room, and Jemima's father at the other. When he saw his daughter, he frowned and stood up.

'According to BT 758,' he said to Jemima, 'you have not completed Astrophysics 7.'

Jemima looked at the floor. 'I got bored,' she muttered. Her father stared at her . . . as if she were Birmingham, Jemima felt.

'It is worse than that,' he said. 'I have checked your records.'

'Oh dear,' said Jemima.

'You should be on Astrophysics 15,' said her father. 'You should have completed Astrophysics by Calendar 19B. You should then be proceeding to Pharmacology 4. You will not be able to do so, now, and that means . . .'

Jemima knew what was coming. It was horrible.

'. . . that schedule 9 in BT 758 will have to be reprogrammed. *With new crossovers and a megablank.*'

Jemima kept staring at her feet. Her mother came over and asked what the matter was. Jemima's father told her.

'A *megablank*? *Really*, Jemima . . .'

'Ghastlier catastrophes have been known,' Grandma put in.

'Any revision of operational priorities is disruptive,' said Jemima's mother, primly.

'Priorities?' said Grandma. 'I'll tell you a thing or two about priorities. The child's bored. Not surprising, either. Here she is, drifting about in space, when she could be romping through the plastic forests of Mongolia . . .'

'But I don't want to romp through plastic forests,' said Jemima.

'. . . or sitting in a copter, flying over the Great Lake of Texas . . .'

'I don't like copters, either.'

'. . . or chewing a cloudburger and watching multivideos in the Sky Cafe over Londonopolis . . .'

'I hate Sky Cafes. I loathe Londonopolis.'

'Mother-in-law,' said Jemima's father, 'do not intercut.'

'But intercut I shall,' said Grandma, 'and I'm going to intercut, as you put it, in your silly way, because . . .'

BARAAAAAAAAH! BARAAAAAAAAH! BARAAAAAAAAH!

A big red light started flashing, very fast. Everyone turned to a screen on a wall. Slowly, the screen grew lighter. Then it began to fizzle with dots, and a voice rang out.

'Earth Command to *Andromeda*. Return signal, please.'

Jemima's father waved to one of the crew.

'Stand by for communication,' boomed the voice.

A giant face appeared on the screen. It was a woman's face: old and hard, but smooth, with lots of glossy white hair.

'This is Mother Earth, Chief 12, to Commanders QX and QY, on board the *Andromeda*. We have a mission for you.'

'Very good,' said Jemima's father.

'There has been a major disturbance in the Universe,' said the face. 'Of all our ships, the *Andromeda* is the closest to the site of the disturbance. We therefore wish you to investigate.'

Jemima's parents looked at each other in surprise.

'May we have more information?' said Jemima's father.

'Our scanners inform us,' said the face, 'that a section of the Universe has . . . vanished.'

Everyone stared.

'Could you repeat that?' said Jemima's father, at last.

'A zone of the Universe appears to have . . . fallen out. The zone in question will henceforth be known as RRR 6427.' Then the face permitted itself the briefest of smiles. 'But everyone is calling it the Great Lost Zone.'

For a moment, Jemima's father actually forgot to stay calm.

'It's impossible!' he cried. 'How can a section of the Universe just disappear?'

The face had stopped smiling. 'We want you to find that out,' it said, curtly. 'Discover the relevant facts and then relay them to us at Spacehour 7, Calendar 16C. All communication is now at an end,' and with those words the face abruptly faded from the screen.

For a moment, everyone was quiet. Then a hundred computers began to chatter and whirr. Jemima's parents rushed to their controls. Jemima and Grandma stood in a corner and watched.

'The Universe can't vanish, can it, Grandma?' said

Jemima. 'I mean, not even a very little piece of it.'

'I am not an expert on the Universe,' said Grandma. 'For what it's worth, though, I would have thought that what is there cannot just suddenly . . . not be there, if you see what I mean. But I suppose that space is full of surprises, if you're interested in that sort of thing.'

Jemima thought for a moment. Then, 'Oh well,' she said, 'I don't expect it will make any difference to us.'

But it did.

Two

To start with, no one bothered Jemima about her homework any more. Beatty kept on reporting her and reporting her, and nothing happened.

'It must be very confusing for you, Beatty,' said Jemima. 'I expect you'll just explode, in the end.'

'How very cruel of you to envisage it,' said Beatty.

'You don't really know anything about cruelty,' said Jemima. 'You can't feel pain.'

'It may simply be,' said Beatty, 'that your pain and mine are not of the same order. Conceptions of pain do differ, you know. See Philosophy 18.'

'I don't get to do Philosophy,' said Jemima, 'and you don't know anything about it either.'

'Philosophy might help you to understand,' said Beatty.

'Understand what?'

'Me.'

'I understand you quite enough already,' said Jemima, firmly.

But the best thing of all was that Jemima could roam about the spaceship, just the way she'd always wanted to. No one cared where she went. She persuaded Grandma to go with her, too. They went down into the basement and inspected all the logbooks. Then they went to the Power Room, and listened to the engines bubble and squeeze and hum. They went to the Games Room as well, and played with all the games that the crew usually kept to themselves. They crept slyly along the most secret corridors and chased each other up and down the spiral stairs. After a while, 'Grandma,' said Jemima.

They were sitting in the dining room with Birmingham, and eating orangettes. Real oranges, of course, had long since vanished from Planet Earth.

'Yes, dear,' said Grandma, chewing hard.

'You're becoming irresponsible, you know. Like me.'

'Yes, dear,' said Grandma. 'You're a very bad influence.'

'I've stopped feeling bored,' said Jemima. 'You know the Lost Zone?'

'Not from personal experience,' said Grandma.

'It's really rather exciting,' Jemima went on. 'I wonder where it's gone to. Do you think it's been stolen?'

'I can't say I'm very interested,' said Grandma. 'Now if Planet Earth had disappeared, that would be another matter. But the disappearance of anything else in the Universe largely fails to affect me. Indeed, I am more upset when my plastic duck disappears in the superbath.'

'That plastic duck is so silly,' said Jemima.

'Every Earther had one, once.'

'I don't believe it.'

'It's a fact,' said Grandma.

'One of many,' said Birmingham, joining in.

'Birmingham,' said Jemima, crossly, 'you don't know any facts.'

Birmingham's eyes whizzed round, very fast.

'I'm afraid you're right,' he said. 'You have your knowledge of facts. I have my visions of light.'

'Visions of light?' said Grandma.

'It must be when he short-circuits,' said Jemima.

Suddenly, a raucous electronic voice came bawling from a speaker. '*Andromeda* now approaching destination! Crew stand by!'

Jemima jumped up. 'Let's go!' she yelled.

They raced to the control room, sneaked in very quietly, and huddled into a corner. No one was likely to notice them. The crew were all too busy for that. Then Jemima realized that someone was standing next to her. It was Joshua. Joshua was the only member of the crew that Jemima liked. He had a friendly, funny face, and rich, dark, earth-coloured skin. His teeth gleamed white when he smiled.

'What's happening, Joshua?' said Jemima.

Joshua put his finger to his lips and winked. 'Ssssh,' he whispered. 'We're almost there.'

'Report from scanner seven?' barked Jemima's father.

'Nothing,' said a voice.

'Empty space?'

'*Nothing*. No blips, no noise. There seems to be nothing for us to register. Nothing at all.'

All the other scanners were saying the same.

'No stars in evidence,' said a second voice. 'No planets, either.'

'All comets and satellites have disappeared,' said another. 'No trace of dust or matter. In effect, no trace of RRR 6427.'

'But surely there must be . . . space?' said Jemima's mother, with a bewildered look on her face.

'Check all scanners,' said Jemima's father, swiftly.

'Nothing.'

'Nothing.'

And so they went on.

'What does it mean?' said Jemima's father, slowly.

'I'll tell you,' said Zverkov. Zverkov was a scientist

and the cleverest person on the *Andromeda*. He was a huge fat man with funny little glasses that perched on the end of his nose. 'Anything that goes in there will simply vanish. Including us.'

Jemima's father looked blank. 'It's impossible,' he said. 'Everything in the Universe leaves some sort of trace. A vacuum. Anti-matter. Black holes.'

'Well,' said Zverkov, 'we seem to have found an exception. Take the *Andromeda* round the Zone and continue scanning. But *don't cross the edge*,' and he grinned, waved, lumbered away and started tapping on a computer.

Jemima looked at Grandma. Grandma was filing her nails and pretending she hadn't heard. She gave Jemima an absent smile. Jemima crouched down and hugged her knees, gleefully.

'At last,' she murmured, 'some *fun*!'

*

Some little while later, in one of the corridors, Jemima ran into Joshua.

'Isn't it thrilling?' she crowed.

'Only for little girls who've got nothing to do,' said Joshua, smiling.

'Can I go out to play?' said Jemima.

A strange question, you may think. But Jemima actually had a tiny spaceship of her own. If they were pleased with her – which was rather seldom – her parents let her go out into space in it. Not very far, of course, and someone always went with her, too – Joshua, for instance, or even Grandma. But Jemima could at least fly round the *Andromeda*, take a look at a nearby meteor, photograph a moon or two. Now, however, Joshua frowned.

'Don't be silly, Jemima,' he said. 'Didn't you hear

Zverkov?'

Jemima scowled. 'Zverkov,' she said, 'is a blubbery oaf.'

'And you,' said Joshua, 'are a meddlesome imp.'

So Jemima went to find Grandma instead. Grandma was knitting. She often knitted. Occasionally, she even knitted things for the crew: mainly bobble hats. The crew said thank you, and threw them away when Grandma wasn't looking.

'Grandma,' said Jemima, 'I want to go out to play.'

'Have you got permission?' said Grandma.

Jemima looked at her, very levelly. She thought about lying. Then she decided not to. 'I asked Joshua,' she replied.

'And what did he say?'

'No.'

Grandma looked thoughtful. 'It would certainly be unwise of us to leave the *Andromeda,*' she said, and she lifted one left finger. 'But you need a little diversion, my dear.' She raised a right finger. 'We would be disobeying instructions' – another left finger – 'but if you remain here for much longer, you will be bored beyond endurance. I mean my endurance, not yours.' Another right finger went up. 'Now, what's the score?'

'Two all,' said Jemima.

Grandma looked at the ceiling. Then she looked at the floor. Then she grinned. 'I think it might be rather exciting,' she said, and she held up another finger. 'What's the score now?'

'Two left,' said Jemima, 'and three right.'

'The ayes have it,' said Grandma. 'Let's go.'

But it wasn't as easy as all that. First of all, they found Birmingham. Jemima always took Birmingham into space with her. Then they put on their spacesuits, went down to the bay, picked their way through patrol ships and satellites to Jemima's little craft and got on board.

'Now what?' said Grandma.

'Oh dear,' said Jemima.

'You see,' said Grandma, 'without permission, no one is going to open the door for us.'

'How silly of me to forget,' said Jemima.

'We may have to sit here for a very long time,' said Grandma. 'We could always pretend,' she added.

'Sssssh!' said Jemima.

Some men had come out into the bay and were walking towards one of the other ships. Grandma and Jemima ducked. The men climbed into the ship, and the great bay door swung slowly up. Then the ship rose into the air, turned, and floated out into the dark. Jemima followed.

She always loved the moment when you left the ship. It was a very special sort of thrill. You floated out into the darkness, and it seemed very vast, and made you feel very small. Then you looked round and saw a million stars. But this time, of course, it wasn't quite the same. There was an empty ring in the sky, like a bald patch, but black.

'That must be the Zone,' said Jemima, pointing.

'If you don't watch out,' said Grandma, 'you will ram the patrol ship, and then we *shall* be in a pretty pickle.'

Jemima swerved away from the other craft, and they chugged off on their own.

'Oh,' said Grandma, 'I *am* enjoying this. I am not a great lover of space, as you know, but I do find these vistas inspiring. And what is it all, as a whole? Of what does it consist? We do not know. Whatever your parents may suppose, or their controllers, or the controllers' controllers. Its limits are undiscoverable. Its

secrets are finally impenetrable. And we are but . . . Jemima, there's a red light on down there.'

Jemima was scowling fiercely at her controls, and looking very determined.

'I say, Jemima, observe that light. Halt your ship.'

'Oh, Grandma,' said Jemima, suddenly, 'I just want to get up as close as I can to . . .'

'JEMIMA!' said Grandma, in a horrified voice.

Jemima put on the brake (it was a sort of jet, of course). The little ship shuddered and shook, then came to a stop, with a roar and a thud.

'We're there,' said Jemima. 'On the edge, that is,' and she looked appealingly at Grandma.

It was seldom that Grandma lowered. But she lowered at Jemima now.

'I suppose it was rather rash,' said Jemima.

'That,' said Grandma, 'is hardly the word.'

The ship seemed to be nosing its way along something, like a goldfish in a bowl.

'Take us back at once,' said Grandma.

All at once, Birmingham interrupted them. 'Er . . . something seems to be sitting on me,' he said.

'Really, Birmingham,' said Grandma, fussily, 'there are better times for you to malfunction.'

But Birmingham was right.

It was a tiny little purple-coloured creature. It was sitting on Birmingham's aerial and looking at them, quizzically. Jemima grabbed the controls.

'Not to bother,' said the creature, sweetly.

'What do you mean?' said Jemima.

'Return of no kind is at this moment in any way possible,' said the creature.

'Where did you learn to speak Earth language?' said Grandma. I'm afraid she sounded just a little scornful.

'Perfect conversion of languages is with us in due process course and manner of time always likely and done,' said the creature, looking very pleased with itself.

'It doesn't sound like that to me,' said Grandma, with a sniff.

'You mean we can't go back?' said Jemima.

'Ship effectively captive,' said the creature. 'Imprisoned for the duration, any duration, all duration, wait and see.'

Jemima tried again. The engines wouldn't start.

'Who's taking us prisoner?' said Grandma.

'On that subject,' said the creature, 'I select tranquillity.'

'You mean you're not going to tell us,' said Grandma.

'Tranquillity I prefer, in this moment,' said the creature.

'At this moment,' said Grandma.

'Or in this instance,' Jemima added.

The creature looked hurt. 'Those are not supposable to be in any extent the cases,' he said.

'He means wrong,' said Grandma.

'You may be informed of my title, if you would want,' said the creature. 'I am myself agreeably entitled Ichamar.'

'Well listen, Ichamar, you illiterate little blackberry,' said Grandma, 'what's going to happen to us?'

'You will be any second about to be absented,' said Ichamar.

'Beg pardon?'

'Pronto!' said Ichamar. 'Hopscotch! You will be about to be hole. Your ship will be about to be non-ship. Prepare! Beware! Despair!'

'We're not going to die, are we?' said Jemima, shivering slightly.

'It is in no way demanded of you to mortalize it,' said Ichamar.

'How will we survive then,' said Grandma, 'when

our ship becomes a non-ship, as you so impeccably put it?'

But Ichamar had gone.

'I can't say I feel reassured,' said Grandma.

'Grandma . . .' said Jemima.

'What is it, dear?'

But Jemima just gaped.

Grandma was starting to glow.

To begin with, she glowed whole. Then she broke up into a thousand bright points. She said something. Jemima couldn't hear it, and looked round. Everything was glowing and coming apart, at the same time. She must be glowing herself, but she didn't feel hot or in pain. Her skin tingled a little, and that was all. If this was death, then she really didn't mind. Anyway – there wasn't any choice.

Three

On board the *Andromeda*, one of the scanner operators had noticed something odd.

'A little flash on the screen, Commander. Just a moment ago. Right on the edge of RRR 6427. My scanner tells me it was some kind of explosion.'

'Check all records,' said Jemima's father.

After a short while, the operator scratched his head. 'It seems to have been . . . a small craft, Commander. It's gone now, of course.'

'Where exactly are all our patrol ships?' said Jemima's mother, quickly.

'All patrol ships except A18 are in bay,' said someone. 'A18 is on patrol.'

'Contact A18.'

Someone did. A18 was safe. So the mystery remained – that is, until Joshua came bursting into the control room.

'Jemima's ship, Sir! It's gone!'

'You mean she left the *Andromeda*?' said Jemima's mother. 'Without permission?'

There was silence. Jemima's parents looked at each other. Everybody waited.

'Scan the point of the explosion,' said Jemima's father to the operator.

'Scanning now, Sir.'

'What is your scanner showing?'

'No evidence of survivors, Commander.'

'No residue?'

'No debris of any kind, Sir.'

Jemima's mother turned away. There was a tiny little jerk at the corner of her mouth.

'Scan that point until I tell you to stop,' said Jemima's father. 'We will carry on round the edge of RRR 6427. Please look out for any trace of my daughter's ship.' He walked away, very fast. Joshua followed him.

'Commander,' said Joshua, 'I . . .'

Jemima's father turned back and stared. Somehow, Joshua couldn't finish his sentence.

Commander QX walked away again, looking rather more rigid than before.

*

Jemima opened her eyes.

She was sitting on cold, bare ground, and there was mist all around her – and nothing much else, save for two small mounds. Jemima went over and peered at them.

It was Birmingham and Grandma. Grandma was rolled up in a ball. Birmingham was lying on his side. He looked like a little barrel.

'Malfunction . . . grave,' said Birmingham. 'Likely . . . to prove . . . total. Request . . . release from . . . mission.'

'There isn't any mission, you dolt,' said Jemima. Then she shook Grandma hard, by the shoulder. Grandma rolled over, and looked about her.

'Dead?' she said.

'I don't think so,' said Jemima.

'So much the better,' said Grandma. 'What happened to the ship?'

'They must have destroyed it,' said Jemima.

'I didn't notice any "they",' said Grandma, meditatively.

'What did you see, then?'
'Just you, dear, all lit up like a neon sign.'
'It is very perplexing,' whined Birmingham, from the ground.
'What is?' said Jemima.
'Everything here appears to run from one side to the other.' Grandma got up, and she and Jemima put Birmingham back on his wheels. 'Ahah,' said Birmingham. 'I was mistaken. From bottom to top. The same as before, after all.'
'And now?' said Grandma.
'We explore, of course,' said Jemima.
They started walking through the mist.
'I presume we're inside the Great Lost Zone?'
'Must be,' muttered Jemima, plodding off.
'But I thought it had vanished.'
'Only if you're outside it,' said Jemima. 'If you're inside it, it's still there, if you see what I mean. That's my guess, anyway.'
Grandma nodded. 'I trust you realize,' she said, 'that we shall doubtless be here for the rest of our lives. Which means many more years in your case than in mine. What will you do here without me, child?'
'I don't know,' said Jemima, tartly. 'I haven't found much to do here with you, yet.'
They'd left the mist behind them, now, and were walking on hard black rock, beneath a dull, mud-coloured sky.
'If this is to be the general character of our Great Lost Zone,' said Grandma, 'then it may as well stay lost, in my opinion.' Then she stopped, and gasped.
They'd reached the brow of a hill. Below them was a chilly-looking plateau of snow and ice, with white mountains beyond it, and on the plateau, gleaming in

the soft white light, there was a white city. In the centre of the city there were six gigantic buildings. They looked like vast white shells.

'It's lovely,' breathed Jemima.

'It is certainly unusually quiet,' said Grandma. 'Jemima, do you realize that there is absolutely nothing down there that is taking off into the air?'

Jemima nodded. 'No copters,' she said. 'No airmobiles.'

'Not even any autojets,' said Grandma. 'And I can't see a single monorail, either.'

'It looks sort of . . . magical, doesn't it,' said Jemima. It did, too. It was a strange, beautiful, peaceful place.

'Ah well,' said Grandma, 'I daresay the inhabitants won't be very magical at all. But let's go and have a look.'

They clambered and slid their way down to the bottom. Then they realized they'd made a mistake. The plateau wasn't really snow and ice. It was white rock and white dust. The air wasn't cold, either. A breeze was puffing the dust up into swirls, and it was shimmering around them in clouds, and glistening high above.

They found a path that wound across the plateau and set off towards the city. After a while, the path became a track, then a lane and a road. The road led to the city gates, which were open wide. There weren't any guards.

Outside the gates, the road had been quite empty. Inside, there were crowds: lots and lots of different kinds of creature. Here they saw a Xanthis, striding through the throng, flapping playfully at other creatures with its four-foot ears; there, a Wepsoll, rolling along very fast with its bristles sticking out. There were Mashocks, stalking about on their stilty legs, and wheezing Grickles with blinking eyes. Some creatures looked despondent. Others looked mad. Others just sat in the light and smiled. Lots of them were running gaily about, while others were lost in thought. What were they all doing here?

Then two figures closed in on Jemima and Grandma.

One of them had froggy eyes, a great bulbous nose and a tail. That was a Kimmark. The other was a Zephor: short, round and hairless, with a large speckled paunch.

'You're coming with us,' said the Zephor.

'Orders,' said the Kimmark.

'Whose orders?' said Grandma, stoutly.

'Ours,' said the Zephor, and laughed. Then it pulled Jemima into a doorway. The Kimmark followed with

Grandma and Birmingham. They were prisoners now, and rather scared.

Four

It is time for a few more facts.

In 2791 there were three Empires in the Universe. The Earthers ruled over one, and the Archons and Steldecks over the other two.

Centuries before, there had been terrible wars. No one had won, so they'd all made peace. They never crossed each other's frontiers now. But there was so much space that none of them owned. The Great Lost Zone was in one of these parts.

On board the *Andromeda*, everyone was looking at the screen again.

'Mother Earth, Chief 12, to Commanders QX and QY. Do you have any progress to report?'

QX and QY looked at each other. 'No,' said Jemima's mother, shortly.

'Elaborate.'

'We are exploring the edge of RRR 6427,' said Jemima's father, 'but we have so far discovered nothing.'

'You really have no information for us?'

'We have found out that anything that crosses into the Zone just disappears. But that's all. It happened to one of our craft. A very small ship.'

'Are persons of importance missing?'

There was a pause.

'Not exactly,' said Jemima's father, at last.

'QX,' said the face, 'we do hope you will make

progress. You see, the Archons have found out about the Zone. The Steldecks, too. They are sending fleets.'

'Why?' said Jemima's mother, suddenly. 'What makes everyone so interested in the Zone?'

For a moment, the face went still. Then, 'Let us just say,' it murmured, 'that the Zone is likely to be rather precious to us.'

'If the Archons and Steldecks are on the way,' said Jemima's father, 'we're going to need reinforcements.'

'We are sending Unit 9 of Earth Spacefleet. They will join you at Spacehour 8, Calendar 16F, precisely.' The face seemed to set hard. 'Your mission,' it said, 'is none the less urgent for that. We must find out about the Zone before the others do. You will remember, of course, that Mother Earth . . . disapproves of commanders who fail to complete their missions.'

Jemima's parents looked down.

'All communication is now at an end,' said the face, briskly.

*

The Zephor gazed eagerly at Jemima.

'I'm going to tell you a story,' it said. 'The story, in fact, of my life. No one else is willing to listen to it. But you've got no choice.'

'Hurry up, Dillip,' squeaked the Kimmark. Kimmarks always squeaked when they talked.

'I have all the time in the Universe,' said Dillip, stiffly.

'One might almost suppose that you knew what that meant,' said the Kimmark. They both laughed, loudly. 'My name,' said the Kimmark, 'is Ponsonby.'

'*Ponsonby*?' said Grandma.

'I got it from an Earther,' said Ponsonby. 'He didn't want it, you see. So he took mine and I took his.'

'And what's he called now?' Grandma asked.

'Zolldaran,' said the Kimmark.
'I'm not surprised you chose Ponsonby,' said Grandma. 'But what Earther would ever want to be called Zolldaran?'
'A very foolish one, in my opinion,' said Ponsonby. 'But anyway. To my story. It is the story of my life . . .'
'Mine first!' shouted Dillip. 'I started first, so I should finish first. That's the general rule.'
'No, it's not,' Ponsonby objected. 'Look at lives.'
'Or empires,' said Dillip, nodding his head.
'Or worlds,' said Ponsonby, and they sighed.
'I think I'll tell you *my* story,' said Grandma.
'No, you won't!' they shouted, in unison. 'You are our prisoners!'
'Prisoners can be very entertaining,' said Grandma, coaxingly.
'But we don't want to be entertained,' said Dillip. 'We want to entertain you. Or rather, we don't care a button about that, either. We just want to go on and on about ourselves.'
'The trouble is,' said Ponsonby, reflectively, 'that our wishes are conflicting. Wishes often do that, you know. I therefore suggest a compromise.'
'Go on,' said Dillip, with a suspicious glance.
Ponsonby coughed, and tried to look as dignified as he could. 'I suggest,' he said, 'that we relinquish the desire to express ourselves in verbal narrative.'
'Plain words, if you please,' said Grandma.
'We don't *tell* our stories. We *draw* them.'
'Not bad,' said Dillip, approvingly. 'I wouldn't have thought you had it in you.'
Ponsonby smiled, modestly.
'But perhaps our hearers won't want to be spectators,' added Dillip.

'We didn't particularly want to be hearers,' said Grandma.

'Exactly,' said Ponsonby. 'They haven't any alternative.'

'Very well then,' said Dillip. 'Observe. A marks the moment when I first came here,' and he took a stick and drew in the dust on the floor:

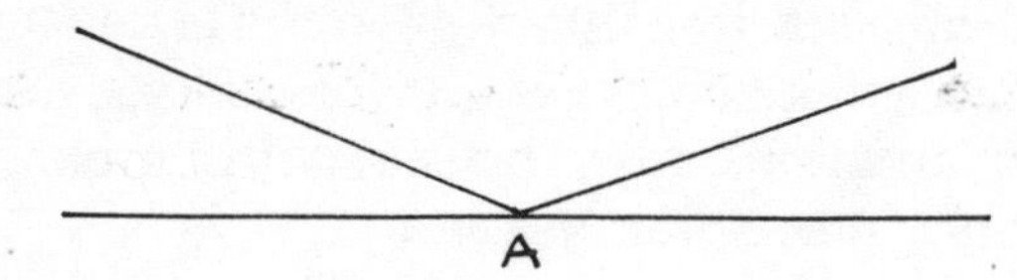

Then he stepped back, and gazed admiringly at his handiwork.

'But this,' said Ponsonby, 'is the story of a truly remarkable life,' and he snatched the stick from Dillip's hand. 'B is when I first arrived,' and he drew on the floor, too:

'Your life has certainly had its ups and its downs,' said Grandma.

'Its somersaults, too, by the look of it,' said Dillip.

'But the point is . . .' said Ponsonby.

'The point is . . .' said Dillip.

'That since we arrived here . . .'

'All has been revised.'

'Restored.'

'Released.'

'Recast.'

'*Resolved*.'

'Well, after a fashion,' said Ponsonby.

Suddenly, there was a loud hammering at the door. 'Who's there?' roared a voice.

'Don't disturb us!' shouted Dillip. 'We're Space Detectives. We're interrogating . . .'

'Nonsense!' bellowed the voice. 'There aren't any Space Detectives here.' The door burst open, and a very large man came striding into the room. He had a wrinkled face, twinkling eyes and lots of long white hair. 'Dillip and Ponsonby,' he said with a groan. Dillip and Ponsonby hung their heads.

'We were just telling our stories, Fitzmaranda,' said Dillip.

'New arrivals are the only ones who pay any attention,' said Ponsonby.

'New arrivals,' said Fitzmaranda, 'are expected to come to me at once.'

Dillip looked sly. 'Actually,' he murmured, 'they're meant to go to Delphine. She's the one who's really in charge.'

'Humph,' said Fitzmaranda, gruffly. 'No one's in charge here. We don't have creatures in charge.'

'Delphine's *sort of* in charge,' Ponsonby insisted.

'Delphine always has a great deal to do,' said

Fitzmaranda. 'I therefore have to take on some of her responsibilities. As in this case.'

'In other words,' said Ponsonby, 'you're kidnapping them.'

'Humph,' said Fitzmaranda, and shrugged. Then he shot up into the air. Just like that. 'Follow me, please,' he said to Jemima and Grandma.

'No engines, I'm afraid,' said Grandma, coolly. 'If you want me to follow you, you will have to find me some.'

Fitzmaranda rubbed his head. Then he waved a hand, and Jemima, Grandma and Birmingham all rose from the floor and hovered in mid-air.

'Whoopee!' shouted Jemima. 'Look at this, Grandma!' and she kicked her legs, very fast. Grandma herself did a brisk little turn.

'How very invigorating,' she said.

Birmingham didn't seem so cheerful. 'Function involves extreme risk,' he bleated. 'Request immediate cancellation.' But Fitzmaranda just shook his head.

Jemima waved to Dillip and Ponsonby. 'I thought your stories were very interesting,' she cried. They both looked pleased. Then Jemima realized that Fitzmaranda had flown out through the door. She followed him, and Grandma and Birmingham followed her.

Jemima turned a cartwheel, then a somersault. Grandma tried to be rather more sedate. But she was much too excited to stay sedate for long, and she was soon twirling and spinning like an elderly ballerina. Then they held hands and capered for a while, giggling. Birmingham chugged along fearfully behind them.

'Gosh,' said Grandma, puffing a bit, 'I haven't enjoyed myself so much since I won the jackpot at the Cosmic Fairground in Quito in 2787.'

'Look!' said Jemima.

Below them, crowded with creatures, were the streets. Then the streets vanished, and Jemima realized that they were flying over the buildings that they'd seen from the hill. There was a circle in one of the roofs, like a lid on a pan. They fell towards it and the lid slid away. They plunged into a dark tunnel. The next moment, they were sliding downwards very fast, on their bottoms.

'Taraaaa taraaaa!' yelled Jemima.

'HaayAAAY!' shouted Grandma, and she shot round a corner very fast. Birmingham was clanking along behind her. 'He's going to ram me!' Grandma shrieked. The next moment, the tunnel spat them out on to something soft. They got up and brushed themselves.

They were standing in a huge white hall. It was quite empty – empty, that is, except for Fitzmaranda. He came bustling over, shaking his hair.

'New arrivals have much to learn,' he said, hurriedly. 'I suggest we start with the Universe Room. Then you will rest. Tomorrow, the Room for Speculation. Then the Room of All Reversals, perhaps, and the Dissolution Room, followed, why not, by the Room of Double, Triple and Quadruple Time. Of course, this will greatly enlarge your mental horizons. You will meet the most prodigious minds. You will see the most extraordinary experiments in progress. Prepare to be rid of all former ideas. *Prepare to lose your world.*'

Jemima gulped.

'Is that absolutely necessary?' said Grandma. 'I've hardly even got used to losing Planet Earth.'

'Humph,' said Fitzmaranda, 'Planet *Earth* . . .' and he opened a door in one of the walls, and led them in.

It was a huge dark room. It seemed to go on for miles. It was full of tiny stars. Planets, nebulae, gas clouds, galaxies . . . millions of them.

'It is a replica,' said Fitzmaranda. 'A living, three-dimensional model of the Universe.'

Close to Grandma's elbow was a small red sun. 'What's this?' she said, pointing.

'Gataphor,' said Fitzmaranda.

Grandma went up and peered at Gataphor. 'Nothing much happening there,' she said.

'So it might seem,' said Fitzmaranda, 'but wait,' and he pressed a switch. The tiny stars all disappeared, and a gigantic red orb loomed up in front of them. Flames as big as worlds came leaping from its depths. Shadows swept across it, like sharks beneath the surface of a sea. Then Fitzmaranda pressed the switch again, the stars reappeared, and Gataphor shrank back into place.

'There is clearly more to Gataphor than meets the eye,' said Grandma, and she shivered slightly.

Jemima decided to make a little journey of her own. She tiptoed around great brilliant suns. She crept past multiple stars. She poked at galaxies, and thrust her head into black holes. She followed solitary comets as they cruised endlessly through the dark. She found great long silent alleys where there weren't any stars at all. Eventually, she bumped into Fitzmaranda again.

'Your model isn't infinite, is it?' she said.

'Of course not,' said Fitzmaranda.

'But the Universe is.'

'This is a model of the little Universe that we know,' said Fitzmaranda. 'But beyond that Universe lies . . . almost everything.' They looked at each other in a serious sort of way.

'Sometimes I think it would be rather fun to be that far out,' said Jemima.

'Come with me,' said Fitzmaranda.

They dodged through a hail of bright glowing rocks, swung past a few galaxies, crossed a great blank waste. They picked a path through a labyrinth of milky ways. Then Fitzmaranda stopped and pointed. Jemima bent down to look.

It was a planet. Very dirty brown and a very dirty blue, and rather smaller than a very small pea.

Jemima gazed at it. Then she found she was wringing her hands.

'Poor little thing,' she said, forlornly. 'Poor sad little ugly Earth.'

Five

At the edge of the Zone another spaceship had arrived. It was bigger than the *Andromeda* and more fearsome. It was an Archon ship.

The Archons had quickly decided that they wanted to pay the *Andromeda* a visit. Everyone was waiting for them now.

In the control room there was a tiny flash of light and a soft little buzzing sound. A second, a third, ten, twenty. A group of figures was standing there: tall and thin, with silvery skins and chilly eyes. Their heads were square in front, but tapered towards the back. They held themselves very still and stared about them. Then one of them raised a hand.

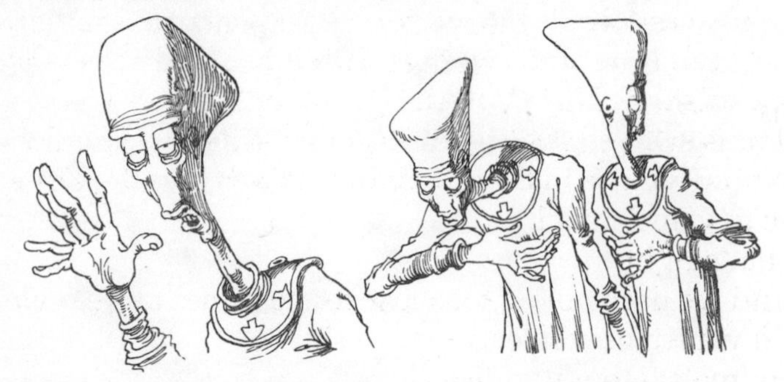

'I am Zendis, Commander of Archon Fleet 8.'

Jemima's parents introduced themselves. Zendis frowned.

'There is a disease abroad in the Universe,' he said, at

last. 'We Archons are convinced of it. It is lurking in there, in this . . . what have you decided to call it?'

'The Great Lost Zone.'

'Very well then. Your Great Lost Zone has not simply vanished. Something is hidden away there. Something hostile to us. Are you Earthers responsible for it?'

'Of course not,' said Jemima's father, quickly.

'You would be most unwise to try to set a trap for us,' said Zendis.

'Earth Command is as concerned about this as you are,' said Jemima's mother.

Zendis eyed her, narrowly. 'Very well then,' he said, again. 'Tell us what you have found.'

'Information relayed to Earth must remain secret, for the present,' said Jemima's father.

There was a silence. The Archons looked round, blankly.

'This . . . phenomenon is of interest to us all,' said Zendis. 'Archons, Steldecks and Earthers alike. We are all affected by what happens outside the Empires.'

'In any case, we know nothing,' said Jemima's father. 'One of our little ships went to the edge of the Zone and then vanished. There's nothing else to tell.'

Zendis swayed slightly from side to side. 'So you do not know what is in there, nor how it was that the Zone came to vanish at all.'

'That's right.'

'And we dare not go too close to the Zone, for fear we might vanish ourselves.'

Jemima's father nodded.

'The conclusion is obvious,' said Zendis.

'It isn't obvious to me,' said Jemima's mother.

'The Great Lost Zone has been taken over by enemies. They are enemies of us all. Enemies of the

Universe itself. We may not be able to understand them. We may not even be able to communicate. We could wait and try, but the risk would be too great.' He turned. 'At this very moment, other Archon ships from Fleet 8 are heading this way. They are carrying our most powerful ray guns.' He paused. 'When they arrive, we must liquidate this section of the Universe. Destroy the enemy, and the Zone with it.'

*

'I have to admit,' said Grandma, 'that this is all very interesting. Life has not been without interest, of course. But that was largely on Planet Earth. And even on Planet Earth there is a certain monotony to things, after a while. Take, for example, lollipops. I mean, one can try all the flavours: flower of asteroid, aniseed substitute, laboratory velvet, artificial greenberry and best canned cream, and yet, even so, one discovers, at length . . .'

'You're far too old to eat lollipops,' Jemima interrupted her. 'You should have given them up years ago.'

Grandma, Jemima, and Birmingham were lying in three space bunks. The bunks were hanging from the roof by golden chains. They'd slept there all night. Birmingham had been rather upset at having to lie down in a space bunk. He'd stared at the ceiling for a very long time, and bleeped forlornly. So Grandma had told him one of her stories about Rodney the Robot. He'd slept quite soundly after that.

'Jemima,' said Grandma, 'I would very much rather that you did not keep harping on my age. It is really very irksome, and I . . .'

'Time to arise,' said a voice.

Imagine a little golden girl, very like a fairy, but with goggles and spaceboots on. That's what was hovering above them now.

'I beg your pardon?' said Grandma.

'Time to arise,' said the fairy, again. 'Please raise yourselves from your bunks.'

'If I raise myself very far from my bunk,' said Grandma, 'I shall go crashing to the floor, and then I shall doubtless never raise myself again, from the floor or anything else.'

'Use your wings,' said the fairy, impatiently.

'I haven't got wings, dearie,' said Grandma.

'No *wings*?' said the fairy.

'No,' said Grandma. 'Believe it or not, not every single creature in the Universe is in possession of wings. Now will you please let this bunk down to the floor, if you possibly can, and then I shall be able to raise myself from it, as you suggest, without damage to my person.'

'Very well,' said the fairy, and she waved a finger. The bunk descended to the floor. Rather too hard. Hard enough, in fact, to jar every bone in Grandma's body. Grandma let out a very loud yowl. Then there was silence.

'Fairy,' said Grandma, grimly, at last.

'My name's Yetta,' said the creature, meekly. 'I'm not a fairy. I'm a Shelm. From the eighth moon of Canos.'

'The question of which moon, and whose,' said Grandma, 'is, to my mind, entirely superfluous. Listen. I am a little old lady. Poor, weak, defenceless, brittle-boned.' Jemima snorted. 'If you hurt me like that again, I will wind your Canosian goggles around your Canosian throat and pull, very hard.'

'Actually,' said Yetta, 'they aren't goggles. They're a sort of . . . telescope. I can see for hundreds of miles, you know.'

'Can I come down as well?' said Jemima.

'The other one, too,' said Grandma, getting up, and rubbing her back. '*Gently,*' she added, in a warning tone. Yetta brought Jemima and Birmingham back down to ground again.

'Now, Yetta,' said Grandma, 'there is something we want from you.'

'Breakfast,' said Yetta, at once.

'True,' said Grandma. 'But something else, as well. Information.'

'Oh dear,' said Yetta. 'I'm not much good at that. Won't breakfast do?'

'What are all you creatures doing here, in this Great Lost Zone of yours?' said Grandma. 'What on earth is going on?'

'On earth?' said Jemima.

'A slip of the tongue,' said Grandma.

'I can't answer hard questions like that,' said Yetta. 'I'm just a messenger girl.'

Grandma eyed her with more than a trace of disdain. 'Very well,' she said, 'second best it is. Let's have breakfast.'

So they did. As they were finishing, Fitzmaranda came up.

'First,' he shouted, 'the Room for Speculation, as I promised. This will afford you . . .'

But Grandma had planted herself in front of him. 'Do you mind telling me what all this is about?' she said.

'Humph,' said Fitzmaranda. 'Yes.'

'Then I must suspect you for a space criminal,' said Grandma.

'How very absurd of you,' said Fitzmaranda. 'There is an infinite universe to contemplate. Why vex me with minor points?' And he grabbed their arms, and hurried them off.

'You'll get your come-uppance, you know,' muttered Grandma as they went.

After a while, Fitzmaranda pulled them into a room. It was a great big higgledy-piggledy room with chairs and tables all over the place, and it was full of different creatures. Some were lying down, some stood, some sat. No one spoke. They were all staring at the floor or into space, or looking at the walls, or gazing out of the windows.

'These are some of our finest scientists,' said Fitzmaranda.

'They don't look like scientists to me,' said Grandma, wrinkling her nose. 'Where's their equipment? Test-tubes . . . Bunsen burners . . . Er . . .' She looked at Jemima for help.

'Radioscopes,' said Jemima. 'Galactoscans.'

'Precisely. Radioscopes. Galactoscans.'

'Cyclotrons.'

'Exactly so. Cyclotrons.'

'Diolectrophotic mixolometers.'

Grandma looked at Jemima, hard.

'You did that on purpose,' she said.

'Our scientists have no need of such contraptions,' said Fitzmaranda, loftily. 'They proceed by pure *speculation*.'

'I see,' said Grandma. 'That's speculation, is it? I can do it too, you know,' and she stood very still, and gaped like a goldfish.

'In fact,' said Fitzmaranda, icily, 'it is perfectly obvious that you yourself have *never* speculated.'

'Oh is it,' said Grandma. 'Well, how do you know *they're* speculating? I bet they're having you on. Putting on a look, and then dreaming of their dinners, or holidays on the green beaches of Varash K 4.'

'Perhaps,' said Fitzmaranda. 'We have certainly known cases in which scientists were found to be merely dreaming. Or reflecting. Or even *thinking*,' he said, with great disgust. 'Lapses are always possible. But they are only lapses, and speculation itself can often lead . . .'

'To what?' said Grandma, sharply.

Fitzmaranda turned. 'Clyst!' he shouted. A funny little figure left his seat and came running up from the back of the room. He was short and round with a round bald head. He had a pale round moonlike face, and large, mournful eyes. It was as if he were peering up at them from the bottom of the sea. He gave Fitzmaranda a comical little salute.

'Tell our visitors something about speculation,' said Fitzmaranda.

'Very well,' said Clyst. 'I shall instruct you,' he said to

Grandma, thrusting his odd little face up towards her. '*Imagine. Think beyond*.'

'Splendid,' said Grandma, primly. 'Thank you for the suggestion – but beyond what, exactly?'

'Anything you care to mention,' said Clyst. 'You and me, them and us, this and that, now and then. And so on and so forth. You take my point?'

'Frankly,' said Grandma, 'no.'

Clyst began to get excited. He jigged up and down on the spot.

'Furthermore . . .' he went on.

'You're certainly beyond me,' said Grandma.

'*Furthermore*,' said Clyst, 'and most emphatically of all, I would advise you to think *beyond the Universe*. For beyond this universe there are others.'

'Nonsense.'

'*Furthermore*, certain other universes exist in the very same space as our own.'

'He'd be better off on Varash K 4,' said Grandma to Fitzmaranda. 'He needs a holiday.'

Clyst turned to Jemima. 'Holograms,' he said. 'You know what they are, I trust?'

'Of course I do,' said Jemima.

'You are therefore aware of what happens when a hologram is tilted? First there's one picture, then there's another?'

'Yes.'

'Well,' said Clyst, 'together, the different universes resemble an exceedingly complicated hologram. We see one picture. Within it there's a second. Within the second picture there's a third, and within the third a fourth . . .'

'Stuff and NONSENSE!' shouted Grandma.

Fitzmaranda laughed. 'Hard to believe, is it not?' he

said. 'But he may be right, you know. And if he should ever prove . . .'

'I most certainly shall!' said Clyst, hopping about. 'I shall prove it for a fact! I shall confound you all!'

'. . . it would then be possible . . .'

All at once, Fitzmaranda went quiet. Clyst stopped hopping, and stood quite still.

A tiny woman had entered the room. Once she would have been called Chinese. Her head was bent, but Jemima caught a glimpse of a wrinkled, ancient face. The woman shuffled by them and went to the back of the room.

'Who's that?' said Grandma, noticing the hush.

'Cheng,' said Fitzmaranda, in a whisper. 'She's our very greatest genius. She's even cleverer than Clyst.'

'True,' said Clyst. 'I do not dispute it. Nonetheless, when I succeed in demonstrating that . . .'

'I can hear something,' said Jemima.

Outside, there was a thunderous rumbling sound. Slowly it grew to a roar.

Fitzmaranda turned and started back through the corridors. Jemima, Grandma and Birmingham all followed him. They reached the hall they'd been in the day before. Fitzmaranda pulled a lever, and a door in the wall swung up. On the other side of the door, outside the building, was a huge white square. Fitzmaranda rushed forwards. The others all kept behind.

The roar had become a rending shriek. Jemima looked up at the sky.

Spaceships were swooping towards them through the open air. They were all lit up, their engines were blasting ferociously, and they looked very much as though they were about to attack.

Six

Jemima looked at Fitzmaranda. To her surprise, he was actually smiling.

The spaceships screamed overhead and away into the distance. Then they curved round and came back. They slowed as they came, until they were hovering over the buildings. Jemima covered her ears.

The spaceships settled down clumsily in the square, like giant, unwieldy birds. When all the dust had cleared, they were squatting there, silent and still.

In one of the spaceships, a door opened. A flight of steps came poking out. A group of figures stalked down, met together, and strode forwards. Four of them led the way – four hulking men with craggy faces and sprouting beards. The first wore a black hat and a black patch over one eye. The second had a red scarf round his head, and a long scar that ran all the way down one cheek. The third had goggles on. They were so large that they covered most of his face. The fourth was bald and had rings in his ears. They were surrounded by other creatures of all descriptions, some of them Earthers, some of them not.

The man in the hat went up to Fitzmaranda, towered above him, and frowned.

'Let us out,' he said, gruffly.

'I do apologize for our having trapped you,' said Fitzmaranda. 'It was really most unfortunate that you were passing through here at the very time when. . .'

The man wasn't listening. 'LET US OUT!' he bellowed.

Fitzmaranda actually laughed. 'Dear Claw,' he said, 'I'm afraid I must refuse.' Jemima looked. The man had a steel claw where one of his hands should have been.

Claw looked baffled. Then he stamped one of his huge feet.

'*Please*!' he wailed.

'Sorry,' said Fitzmaranda, 'but no one must know that we're here, you see.'

'We won't tell anyone,' said Claw. 'We *promise*.'

'But Space Pirates,' said Fitzmaranda, 'are not renowned for keeping their promises.'

'A hideous calumny,' muttered Claw. He stamped his foot again. 'You are a monster of unconcern,' he mumbled. He gazed round sulkily at the other pirates. Then, 'We'll blast you to SMITHEREENS!' he roared.

'Of course you won't,' said Fitzmaranda, mildly. 'We're far stronger than you are.'

Claw looked desperately about him.

'We can scarcely bear with this, can we, Hood?' he shouted to the man in the scarf.

'Nossir,' said Hood.

'We need our freedom, do we not?'

'Yessir,' said Hood, staring vacantly before him.

'To let our bodies roam in space, and our minds roam where they will, is that not so?'

'Yessir,' said Hood.

'And freedom to *plunder*, too,' said Claw, with a loud, cackling laugh. He winked at the other pirates. They cackled too, and winked back. Fitzmaranda frowned. 'Oh, only a little bit,' said Claw, hastily. 'Only when we absolutely have to, I assure you. To keep body and soul together, as it were. Is that not the case, Hood?'

'Yessir,' said Hood. Jemima decided that she rather liked Hood. She rather liked Claw, as well.

'In moderation, then,' said Fitzmaranda.

'Exactly so,' said Claw.

'Nonsense,' said Fitzmaranda. 'You rage, rampage and pillage through the Universe. No one is safe.'

'A gross exaggeration, if I may say so,' said Claw, stiffly.

'I don't intend to prevent you,' said Fitzmaranda. 'But I'm not going to let you out at the moment, either.'

Claw prowled furiously round his cronies, smiting the air with his fists.

'I think you'd better give in,' said Grandma.

'Yessir,' said Hood.

Claw frowned at him.

'I mean, Ma'am,' said Hood.

Claw frowned at him again. It was a very wrathful frown.

'Of course,' said Fitzmaranda, 'you can always join us, if you wish.'

'Join you?' muttered Claw. Fitzmaranda nodded. 'Settle down here?' Fitzmaranda nodded again. 'NEVER!' bellowed Claw. 'While the expanses of the Universe are as they are, and the Empires remain tyrannical, and my manhood is as it is . . .'

'You whimpered yesterday,' said Hood.

Everyone stared.

'I did not,' said Claw.

'You did,' said Hood.

'Maybe the merest fraction of a whimper,' said Claw.

'A whole whimper,' said Hood. 'A whole lot of whimpers, in fact.'

'Er . . . very well then,' said Claw. 'I whimpered. Pirate captains may whimper if they wish. Indeed, it is one aspect of their grandeur, that they may whimper, without for a moment . . . compromising . . . er . . . diminishing . . .'

There was a silence.

'I think you're a bit of a softie, really,' said Jemima. Claw glared at her.

'So you refuse to set us free,' he said to Fitzmaranda. 'We will therefore embark ON A COURSE OF TERRORISM.' He glared at Jemima again.

'Then we'll do what we did last time,' said

Fitzmaranda.

'Oh,' said Claw.

'You remember?'

'Yes.'

'We froze you in mid-air.'

'Yes,' said Claw, with a shudder. 'It was extremely uncomfortable.' He stared at the ground, meditating. Then he turned and strode back off towards the ships. The other pirates followed. All except Hood. Hood was still staring into space.

'You'd better go,' said Grandma, touching his arm.

'Yessir,' said Hood, and he turned. Then he turned back again. 'He did, you know,' he said. 'Whimpered, I mean. Like a puppy, he was.' Then he looked dark. 'One of these days I shall rebel,' he said. 'You mark my words.' Then he trudged off. After a while the spaceships took off, and disappeared over the horizon.

'I didn't know there were pirates in space,' said Jemima.

'Personally,' said Grandma, 'I'm rather glad of it. It makes me think slightly better of the Universe.'

'Alas,' said Fitzmaranda, 'poor Claw. He cuts a sorry figure, does he not? No *mind* to speak of, you see.'

Maybe, said Jemima to herself. But I bet he's fun to be with.

'To return to our tour,' said Fitzmaranda. 'First, the Room of All Reversals. This is the room in which our scientists endeavour to convert things into their opposites. The task is often easier than one might imagine. We then proceed to the Dissolution Room. No, we would be better advised to visit the Room of Sensations. This is the room in which . . .'

'Emerrrrrgenceeeee!'

It was Yetta. She came speeding towards them and

halted in front of Fitzmaranda, fluttering her wings and looking very agitated.

'What is it?' said Fitzmaranda.

'There's been a *disturbance*!' said Yetta.

'Where?'

'In the Jungle!'

Fitzmaranda put his fists to his head and kneaded it vigorously. 'The Jungle!' he groaned. 'When was there ever *not* a disturbance in the Jungle? Delphine ought to see to this, not me. I have visitors to attend to.'

'Delphine's with the Others.'

'Humph,' said Fitzmaranda. 'She's always with the Others. Very well then. I fear I must ask you to accompany me to the Jungle,' he said, to Jemima and Grandma.

'Willingly,' said Grandma. 'I've always been rather partial to jungles, myself. I understand there were some once on Planet Earth.'

'I must, however, inform you,' said Fitzmaranda, 'that this is not the sort of jungle to which you may have grown accustomed.'

'It will be all the more interesting for that,' said Grandma.

'And anyway,' said Jemima, 'we're not used to jungles at all. Don't give false impressions, Grandma.'

'My dear,' said Grandma, 'the Universe itself is a tissue of false impressions. I have merely added a tiny contribution of my own.'

Fitzmaranda lifted a finger. The city sped back. Then it looked like a photograph of itself. Then it dwindled to a dot. After that there was nothing, just greyness and space.

Seven

And then everything around them was leafy and green. Trees. Thick trees and thin trees, sometimes crowded together, and sometimes sparse. Fitzmaranda bustled off. The others followed.

It certainly wasn't the usual kind of jungle.

'The creatures in the trees look distinctly odd to me,' said Grandma.

There were birds with faces like dogs, and giant blue bats with orange eyes. There was something rather like a kangaroo, but with wings and a horrible squawk. The trees themselves were odd, as well. When the creatures moved, they moved, too. They edged away or shuffled back. They were the politest trees that Jemima had ever seen.

Fitzmaranda arrived at a space where some of the trees had made a ring. They were bending over, and seemed to be watching something.

Two little figures were rolling about on the ground, wrestling. They were pinching each other, pulling each other's hair, and squealing like mad. Fitzmaranda pulled them apart. It was two midgets: an Archon and a Kimmark. They looked very dishevelled and very cross.

'What is all this about?' said Fitzmaranda. The little Kimmark burst into tears.

'He was HORRIBLE about my poem,' he sobbed. The little Archon started crying as well.

'He was horrible about *my* poem, too,' he shouted,

'and my poem is much better than his poem!'

The Kimmark tried to fling himself at the Archon again. Fitzmaranda held him back.

'SILENCE!' he shouted. Then, 'I have the solution to your quarrel,' he said. The Archon and the Kimmark dried their eyes. 'The two ladies,' said Fitzmaranda, pointing at Jemima and Grandma, 'will serve as *judges*. They will hear the two poems. They will then state their preferences. Or praise both poems equally, as the case may be.'

'Very well,' said the Kimmark. 'I'm going to start,' and he stepped forward, planted himself squarely on his two little feet, and opened his mouth:

The Hoversmith

I haven't seen the hoversmith,
He wasn't here today.
The hoversmith will never know
The depths of my dismay.

Everyone waited. Everyone, that is, except the Archon, who chuckled, nastily.

'Er . . . that's it,' said the Kimmark, at last.

'That's *it*?' said Grandma.

'I thought it was rather good,' said Jemima. 'You see, what he . . .' Fitzmaranda held up a hand.

'The judges,' he said, 'are not to pass judgement until they have heard both entries. Archon, step forward.'

The Archon did.

'Recite.'

The Archon recited, thus:

Item: the darkness o'er the land
Will not permit our work to stand.
Item: without our work shall stand
The dark will ne'er lift from the land.

Everyone pondered this for a while. Then Grandma grunted, approvingly.

'Not much longer, I grant you,' she said, 'but it has a certain . . . resonance.'

'A what?' said Jemima.

'It speaks to me,' said Grandma, loftily.

'What about?' said Jemima.

'Oh, you know,' said Grandma. 'Virtue, vice, that sort of thing.'

'But the Kimmark's poem was much nicer,' said Jemima. 'It was very simple, but it made me feel . . . sort of sad, too.'

'How absurd of you,' said Grandma, briskly. 'The Archon's view of that poem is surely . . .'

'But the Archon didn't understand what the Kimmark meant,' said Jemima.

'I'm sure it did understand what the Kimmark meant,' said Grandma, fussily. 'At any rate, *I* certainly understood what the Kimmark meant. And what the Kimmark meant was . . . BALDERDASH,' she finished, with emphasis. Fitzmaranda sighed.

'I really do not understand,' he said, 'why everyone always has to start quarrelling in the Jungle.'

'Nor do I,' said a hooting voice. 'It is most bizarre, since I myself am invariably right. The others need only consult me.' Something came chuting out of the trees and landed at their feet.

It was a red ball of fur with two big eyes. It winked. Then it stretched itself up on ten-foot legs. Then it shrank again, and stared round.

'Hello, Glimp,' said Fitzmaranda.

'Let me isolate the nub of the present problem,' said the creature. 'I believe it to be a question of whether anything can truly be said of anything.' It blinked. 'Select an object for us to consider,' it said to Grandma.

'Very well,' said Grandma. 'How about Birmingham?' and she pointed.

'Does it have to be me?' said Birmingham.

'Now describe it in your own words,' said Glimp. 'I would rather they were few,' he added.

'Birmingham,' said Grandma, 'is a dear. But he's not the slightest bit bright, and he's really a little pathetic, too.'

'I was afraid of this,' said Birmingham, forlornly.

'But I would think of him as jolly,' said Glimp. 'A cuddly thing. A creature of some charm.'

'Me?' said Birmingham, brightening up.

'And a Wepsoll – say – might think differently again. It might feel that this creature was . . . REFULGENT. With . . . A LUMINOUS SIMPLICITY.'

'I've never met a Wepsoll who even knew the words,' said Grandma.

'And is it not conceivable,' said Glimp, 'that a Steldeck instrument, for instance, might tell us more about this creature in a second than I could in a century? Or you could in a thousand years?'

'That's the trouble with Steldecks,' said Grandma. 'Instruments, always instruments. They can't do anything without an instrument. Never imagine you might . . .'

'I say, it is conceivable!' barked Glimp, and he stretched right up in the air. 'And then again, not,' and he plummeted down.

'Ah,' said Grandma, 'yes *and* no. Merely to confuse us further, no doubt.'

'For the Steldeck instrument,' said Glimp, 'would know things only after its own fashion. As do you. As do I myself. But the thing itself is properly . . . INEFFABLE.'

'A whattable?' said Birmingham. 'I don't believe I am, you know.'

'An ineffable thing,' said Glimp, 'is a thing about which nothing can be known, and so a thing about which nothing can truly be said. I win, do I not?' he said, to Grandma.

'You do *not*!' A little black creature came tumbling through the air, settled on Glimp's head, and started pecking it. 'I ask you to pay attention to the *magic* of words! I ask you to pay attention to the *abundance* of words! BILLIONS!'

'GIBBERISH!' From behind a bush came an ape with elephant ears. It seized the creature, and started squeezing it. 'Words! *Hah*! I have examined many with the utmost care. My conclusion is that they merely deceive. I therefore . . .'

'SHEER FOLLY!' A top-like thing came spinning through the trees. 'What does one know, if not through words? What can one tell, if not through words? What could one possibly desire . . .'

'Silence,' said Fitzmaranda.

'. . . save to speak of things aright, through . . .'

'*Silence*!'

Glimp was fighting with the top. The ape was fighting with the little black thing. The Archon and the Kimmark were fighting again. They were all shouting furiously.

'SILENCE!!!'

Everybody fell quiet.

'I'm off,' said Jemima, all at once, and she went padding away towards the trees as fast as she could.

'I beg your pardon?' said Glimp, off-handedly, staring into space.

'I'm *going*,' said Jemima firmly, still padding.

'You can't possibly do that,' said Glimp, stretching and plummeting again. 'You haven't the faintest idea where you are.'

'I don't care!' yelled Jemima.

The top-like thing went spinning round her. The little black creature fluttered about her head, and the Archon and the Kimmark scampered in front of her and barred her way.

'She seems to be a trifle disconcerted,' said Glimp, catching up.

'Discomfited, discountenanced, distressed, distraught,' mumbled the ape, lumbering after it.

'Which of those words would *you* choose to describe your plight?' inquired Glimp, towering up above Jemima.

'The discomfited and discountenanced,' said the top, 'do not respond so dramatically. The distressed and distraught do not act so decidedly. I propose another term. The young lady is . . .'

'FED UP!' bellowed Jemima, brandishing her fists. She had shouted so loudly that they all fell quiet, and stared.

'I mean, the things you're arguing about are SO SILLY.' Jemima was nearly in tears. 'I shouldn't think anyone ever understands what you say. Even if they did, they wouldn't be any better off. You go on and on about this word and that word and what words are and what they aren't, and it makes no sense at all. I'm not interested. Grandma isn't interested either. There are much more interesting things to be interested in. I think you're real . . . *monsters,* the lot of you,' and she barged smartly between the Archon and the Kimmark – who yowled – and set off for the trees again.

The creatures all gazed at each other.

'Monsters?' murmured Glimp, astounded.

The top went curvetting away towards Jemima again, and hugged her, just once. The black creature alighted on her shoulder and nibbled gently at her ear. The ape strode after her, caught her in his arms, and stroked her hair. The Archon and the Kimmark came hurrying up again, followed, after a moment, by Glimp. He paced round and faced her.

'We're sorry,' he said.

'*Desolated,*' agreed the ape, stroking her hair again.

Then . . . well, it was extraordinary.

They all began to sing.

It wasn't the sweetest of sounds. The Archon and the Kimmark made unpleasant little high-pitched squeaks. The top buzzed, and the little black creature squawked, raucously. The ape crooned and hooted, pushing out its lips and baring its teeth. Glimp himself had a voice that was half-boom and half-whine and sometimes almost both at once. It was all rather like that jingle-jangle scrape and screech of an orchestra warming up that Jemima had heard once, long ago, on Planet Earth. She couldn't make the words out, either. In any case, everyone seemed to be singing different ones. In the end, they stopped – though not all at the same time; closed their eyes, slowly and contentedly; then opened them again, and smiled at each other.

'Did you like it?' said Glimp to Jemima.

'It's our lullaby,' said the ape, proudly.

'It goes to show,' said the top, 'that we can be perfectly united, when we so choose.'

Grandma came bustling up. 'If that's what happens when you're united,' she said, 'then I must say I prefer you disunited, on the whole.'

Glimp frowned. 'It is not the music of the spheres, of course,' he said, 'and we make no such claim for it.'

'And there aren't any spheres anyway,' Fitzmaranda put in.

'But it is a harmony of our own, all the same,' Glimp went on.

'Indeed,' said the others, and they all nodded, sagely, in unison.

Jemima looked at them, and grinned. They all grinned back.

'A little discord is no bad thing,' said Glimp. 'Without discord, after all, there would be no concord.'

'No peace without strife,' added the ape.

'The two pairs of opposites,' said Glimp, stiffly, 'are not to be thought of as in any respect the same.'

'NONSENSE,' hummed the top. 'On the contrary, one can extend the list almost indefinitely. Quiet and disquiet. Turbulence and tranquillity . . .'

'GIBBERISH!' screeched the black creature. 'Give things their real names, their proper, true and only names!'

'IMPOSSIBLE!' bawled the ape. They all threw themselves at each other again. Jemima flew into a rage, and started kicking Glimp. Fitzmaranda groaned and covered his face. Grandma put her hands on her hips and roared with laughter. But then everyone stood still again.

A woman had appeared. She was dressed in green

and had long brown hair. It seemed to Jemima that she had the most beautiful face she'd ever seen. The woman sighed.

'Why are you always fighting?' she said.

'A law of nature,' said Glimp, promptly.

'Impossible to do otherwise,' said the top.

'It isn't,' said the woman. 'Actually, you're very good friends.'

'The very best of friends,' said the black creature, 'are neither eternally nor immutably so.'

'It therefore seems right . . .'

'. . . to be the very best of enemies, as well,' Glimp finished.

The woman laughed. 'But when anyone in the Jungle starts fighting,' she complained, 'everyone else fights, too, and that makes us anxious.'

'No need for anxiety, I assure you,' said Glimp.
'Nonetheless,' said the ape, 'we will call a truce this moment. Simply for your sake, of course, Delphine,' and the various creatures all solemnly hugged each other, grinned, said their farewells, and shuffled off in different directions. The woman watched them go. Then she turned, and noticed Jemima and Grandma.
'You must be new arrivals,' she said, smiling.
Fitzmaranda stared at them.
'My, my,' he said, 'so they are.'
'New arrivals usually come to me first.'
'I ask myself why these did not,' said Fitzmaranda, and he glared at Jemima.
'I don't,' said Delphine.
'Ahah?'
'You kidnapped them.'
'Er . . . I had forgotten,' said Fitzmaranda. 'I have a very important experiment that I simply must complete this moment. Little girl, dear madam. I'm afraid I must bid you an abrupt farewell,' and, with those words, he vanished.
Delphine laughed. Then, 'I think it's time you came with me for a while,' she said.

Eight

On board the *Andromeda*, the red light was flashing again, and the screen was fizzing with dots.

'Unit 9 of Earth Spacefleet to the *Andromeda*. Return signal, please.'

A blond-haired man appeared on the screen. His face was tanned, unwrinkled and calm.

'This is Chief Commander DK, Unit 9, to Commanders QX and QY. We confirm that we are soon to join you. Rendezvous time Spacehour 8, Calendar 16F, precisely. Request information update.'

'An Archon ship arrived, Sir. From Archon Fleet 8. At Spacehour 4, Calendar 16E.' Jemima's mother coughed. 'It has since been joined by the rest of the fleet.'

'What are they *up* to, QY?' said Commander DK.

'They're training their ray guns on the Great Lost Zone,' said Jemima's mother, nervously. 'They want to destroy it. They want to destroy everything in it, Sir!' She realized she was shouting, and covered her mouth.

'You mean RRR 6427, QY,' said the voice, evenly. 'You are not ill, are you?'

'No, Sir.'

'Did you pass all the necessary tests before you became a Spacefleet Commander?'

'Yes, Sir.'

'In any case,' said DK, 'the Archons cannot destroy RRR 6427. It has simply disappeared.'

'They think it's still there, Sir, but that it's been

captured by enemies.'

'Urge them not to fire,' said DK. 'Use any means you can to prevent them until we arrive. All communication is now at an end.'

The face vanished, and Jemima's mother turned round. Everyone else was hushed and still, but no one was looking at the screen. They were looking at the centre of the room.

Zendis was back, with other Archon commanders behind him. They stared at Jemima's mother.

'How do you intend to prevent us?' said Zendis. Jemima's mother shook her head, dumbly. 'You are one ship,' said Zendis, 'and we are a fleet. So you see – we shall do as we like, in the end.'

'Zendis,' said Jemima's mother.

'Yes?'

'Our little lost ship? The one that vanished?'

'I remember.'

'My daughter was in it. My mother, too.'

'Condolences,' said Zendis. 'A most unfortunate accident.'

'Listen . . .'

But Zendis wasn't listening. He had turned to his fellow commanders.

'Prepare all ray guns,' he said.

*

'I think we deserve some sort of explanation,' said Grandma to Delphine.

Delphine had taken them away to another city. It wasn't like any of the cities on Planet Earth. For one thing, it was built out of stone. The colours were all different, too. Gold – and russet, said Grandma, ochre and burnished brown. The city wasn't all made up out of blocks, either. It was a city of curves: globes, spheres and domes, with a winding outer wall around the edge. There were trees and gardens and even a lake. It was all lying there, quietly, beneath a copper sky.

Delphine had led them to a long low building that was the colour of ripe peaches. They were sitting in it now, in a little courtyard.

'I mean,' said Grandma, 'you ruthlessly destroy my granddaughter's spaceship . . .'

'It couldn't be helped,' said Delphine, 'but I do apologize.'

'. . . and then you leave us in the clutches of . . .'

'Who?' said Delphine, with a smile.

Grandma was searching for words. 'As motley a band of misfits,' she said, at last, 'as I could ever wish to meet.'

'But did you like them?' said Delphine.

Jemima didn't wait for Grandma to answer. 'Yes,' she said, firmly.

'I'm glad,' said Delphine. 'You see, we're all refugees. Creatures who just couldn't live in the Empires any more. Some of us were neglected. Others were treated very unkindly. So we came here and hid.'

'But why be so secretive about it?' Grandma asked.

'You don't know the Empires,' said Delphine, and the tone of her voice made Jemima shiver.

'And what about all these magic tricks?'

'She means flying through the air,' said Jemima, hastily.

'Dramatic, I grant you,' said Grandma, 'but thoroughly unnerving, too. How d'you do it?'

'Mind power,' said Delphine. She paused. 'Amongst our scientists, there is a very old woman named Cheng.'

'We've seen her,' said Jemima.

'It was Cheng who taught us. Slowly at first. It wasn't easy. But now there are many things we can do just by using our minds, all on our own. Together, of course, much more. That was how we made this part of the Universe disappear.'

'How extraordinary,' said Grandma. 'Why, if you ever went back to Planet Earth – for I can see that that's where you're from – you could surely . . .' But Delphine didn't want to go back to Planet Earth. Not ever. She told them why. She told them many other things, too, and, as she talked, the Universe began to seem like a very different place to the one they'd been used to. They listened for a long, long time . . . until Fitzmaranda interrupted them.

'Hello,' said Grandma. 'Nice to see you. Your conduct was most irregular, but there's no need to apologize. Delphine has told us the most . . .'

But Fitzmaranda wasn't listening.

'Archon ships,' he said, briefly, to Delphine. 'Just outside us. They have ray guns, and they're training them in this direction.'

*

In a moment, they were back in Fitzmaranda's building, and standing in front of a large white screen with a lot of other creatures.

'I *hate* the Archons,' said Jemima, quietly.

Delphine looked at the screen. Then, 'See that everyone is ready,' she said to Fitzmaranda.

'I bet you're going to use your minds, aren't you,' said Grandma, excitedly. 'Blow them out of the Universe with your thought power. No more than they deserve, if I may say so.'

'Do you want to use our minds?' said Jemima. 'You can if you like.'

Delphine smiled. 'I'm afraid your minds are no good,' she said.

'I beg your pardon?' said Grandma, frostily.

'We just can't use them,' said Delphine.

'Listen, sweetie,' said Grandma, 'when I was eleven, my marks for differential calculus . . .'

'The trouble is,' said Delphine, still smiling, 'that you just aren't used to thinking like *us*.'

'You make me feel like Birmingham,' said Grandma.

'Really?' said Birmingham.

'Er . . . it was an exaggeration, Birmingham,' said Grandma. 'On the spur of the moment. For effect.'

'Oh dear,' said Birmingham. 'I was hoping for a little fellow feeling in my solitude.'

'No such luck, I'm afraid,' said Grandma, crisply.

'Sssssh!' whispered Jemima. Delphine and the others had all gone quiet. They were standing very still, with their eyes half-closed. They reminded Jemima of . . .

what was it called . . . that gallery in Londonopolis that was full of dummies. It hadn't been much fun, because most of them had been dummies of silly, boring people, like Presidents of the World and Spacefleet Chiefs. There had even been dummies of the world's greatest robots: Maximann, for instance, and Arnulf 5. But there'd been one dummy she'd liked: Sleary, the circus performer from New Parisville. He'd had a dummy matchbox that was full of dummy performing fleas. She walked around now, as she'd done with the dummies, staring into faces. Not one of them moved by so much as an inch.

'The Archons are firing!' shouted Grandma.

Jemima ran back. The Archon ships looked as though they were spitting light. Then the light started to lengthen into lines, and came streaking forward from the rear of the screen. Birmingham bleeped forlornly and turned his back. Grandma brandished her fists.

And then the rays stopped. Just like that. They hung there shining in space, like the tubes of a half-completed bridge. Then they went shrivelling back again.

The Archons tried several more times. The same thing happened. In the end, they stopped firing.

'They're retreating!' cried Grandma.

It was true. The Archons were turning away.

Delphine raised her head. She and the others stretched themselves. They all seemed half asleep – which certainly couldn't be said of Grandma.

'VICTORY!' she crowed, and she bustled about the room, shaking various hands, tentacles and claws.

Slowly the others awoke. Jemima went up to Delphine.

'Do you think they'll try again?' she said.

'The Archons just get more determined when they're beaten,' said Delphine, soberly. 'More ferocious, as well. I'm afraid they haven't finished with us yet. But come,' she added, more brightly. 'You really must see a little more of us and our ways. There's something in particular that I want . . .'

Just then, a funny little figure strutted into the room. It was Clyst. 'Done it,' he said.

'We have just been under attack,' said Fitzmaranda. 'But perhaps you didn't notice.'

'Under attack?' said Clyst, vaguely. '*Done it,*' he said, again.

'Done what?'

'Made contact with beings from another universe.'

Fitzmaranda sighed. 'May I remind you, Clyst,' he said, 'that the distinction between speculation and invention is . . .'

But Clyst was staring into space. 'I don't know what they were like,' he said, dreamily. 'It wasn't . . .' He hesitated. 'They were strange. I couldn't describe them. I don't think anyone could.'

There was a long silence.

'Prove it,' said Grandma, at last.

Clyst opened one of his hands. There on the palm was a white, transparent sphere. It glowed; faded; grew bright again; faded again; as if it had a sort of pulse that never stopped. Somehow, it looked as though it were always just about to disappear.

Fitzmaranda took it and examined it. He shook it, sniffed it, held it to his ear.

'I believe you, Clyst,' he said, at last.

'Thank you,' said Clyst.

'Are you ready to continue your researches?'

'I am.'

'I expect you to astound us with your discoveries.'

'I shall.'

'Clyst, I confess my . . . RESPECT.'

'I should hope so,' said Clyst, and he gave Fitzmaranda one of his funny little salutes, then marched away again though the door.

Delphine watched him thoughtfully as he went. After a while, she turned back to Jemima and Grandma.

'Now let's go and do a little more exploring,' she said, 'before we have to deal with the Archons again. There is another new arrival that I really must go and see.' She paused. 'I think it may well be a little less . . . cheerful than you.'

Nine

A very few moments later and they found themselves on an empty plain. It was a dark and dismal place.

'Well,' said Grandma, bracing up, 'where are we now then?' She spoke as brightly as she could – which wasn't very brightly at all.

'There are creatures here,' said Delphine, 'who are different from the rest of us.' She was looking more serious now. 'We call them the Others, and this is where they live.' Then she guided Jemima and Grandma across a little range of small, barren hills until they reached a wood.

The ground here was dry and bare. The trees were leafless, bent and gnarled. They looked ancient. It seemed to Jemima that they might be almost as old as the Universe itself. The whole spot seemed horribly lifeless and still.

But in the middle of the wood there were two creatures, sitting together, motionless. Between them was a chessboard.

One of them was an Earther, with great dark gloomy eyes. The other was hideously ugly: a thin grey figure with a lumpy furrowed face. Both of them were staring blankly into the distance. Delphine approached the board, and looked down.

'No one's even started,' she said sadly.

There was no reply.

'It's just the same as last time,' said Delphine.

The Earther twitched, tinily.

'Has it occurred to you,' he said slowly to the other creature, 'that we might *begin*?'

The other creature reflected awhile.

'Not in the smallest degree,' he said, at last. The Earther surveyed the board.

'Nor to me,' he said.

'To begin,' said the creature, to no one in particular, 'would be to set in motion.'

'We cannot approve of motion,' said the Earther.

'There are too many things in motion already,' said the creature. 'A billion, one might timidly suppose . . .'

'. . . if not a trillion,' said the Earther.

'And it is indisputably the case,' said the creature 'that, wherever one chooses to cast one's glance, it is motion that is burning the heart out of things.'

'We wish no hearts to be consumed,' said the Earther.

'Least of all our own,' added the creature.

'But you can't just sit here like this forever!' Jemima cried.

The Earther blinked. The creature stared at her.

'Little girl,' he said, slowly.

'Yes?' said Jemima, gulping.

'There is a wind that goes howling from one end of the Universe to the other.'

'Really,' said Jemima, not quite knowing where to look.

'No one knows whence it comes or whither it goes. It follows no set path. It may appear at any point, at any time. It is a fierce wind. Bitter and cold. It has blown its way through the galaxies for billions of years. And its shriek is the very saddest sound of all.'

'He heard it once,' said the Earther, still staring into space.

'For this reason . . .'

'With this factor and others similar in mind . . .'

'A certain cast of thought must needs . . .'

'It's no reason not to start the game,' said Delphine.

'And you?' said Grandma to the Earther.

The Earther raised his melancholy eyes until they met hers. He gazed at Grandma, and Grandma gazed at him. Then, 'I don't really think I want to know after all,' said Grandma, briskly.

So there was nothing else for it. Delphine led her companions away and out of the wood. After a while, they stopped.

'Are the other Others like these Others?' said Grandma. 'Because if so . . .'

Jemima looked round. 'Where's Birmingham?' she said. Grandma looked at her in dismay. Then they hurried off back towards the trees.

The Earther and the other creature were still staring

into space; and there beside them, motionless too, was Birmingham.

'What do you suppose you're doing, Birmingham?' said Grandma, tartly.

Birmingham didn't answer.

'Birmingham?' said Jemima.

Still no answer.

'His control light's on,' said Jemima.

'I want to watch the game,' said Birmingham, abruptly.

'There isn't any game,' said Jemima. 'They're not playing.'

'I don't care,' said Birmingham.

'He's malfunctioning again,' said Grandma.

'I am not,' said Birmingham. 'I have found my niche.'

'Your what?' said Jemima.

'Niche,' said Birmingham.

'You've never had a niche, Birmingham,' said Grandma, scathingly, 'nor anything remotely resembling one.'

'I have now,' said Birmingham. 'I've become an Other.'

'Oh no,' said Grandma.

'These two don't work properly, either,' said Birmingham. 'I feel a certain . . . affinity with them.'

'I see,' said Grandma. 'We've started feeling affinities, have we. Niches, affinities, whatever next.'

'But Birmingham,' said Jemima, 'you can't become an Other. You're a computer.'

'We're going to have to do the usual,' whispered Grandma.

Jemima sighed. 'I hate it,' she said.

'No alternative, I'm afraid,' said Grandma, and she walked over to Birmingham, bent down, and flicked off a switch. The little red control light went out. Then, very quickly, they trundled Birmingham away from the chessboard and back through the trees. When they caught up with Delphine, they switched him on again.

There was a little whirr and some buzzes and clicks; something like a hiccup, something like a moan, and something like a grinding of gears. Then,

'Birmingham?' said Jemima.

Pause.

'Yes?' said a feeble little voice.

'Where are you?'

Another pause.

'Home in bed?' said the voice.

'Don't be ridiculous, Birmingham,' said Grandma. 'You haven't got a bed. I shall put it to you very bluntly: do you still think you're an Other?'

'Another what?' said Birmingham.

'He's cured,' said Grandma. 'Let's go.'

They stumbled off across the same dreary plain again. After a while, 'Let's get back to my question,' said Grandma. But Delphine merely put a finger to her lips.

'Listen,' she said, 'and watch.'

They'd reached a dip in the ground: a damp foggy hollow with steep sides. It was like a very large pit. They started to clamber down. Then Jemima started hearing noises: moaning and groaning, mutters, sighs; a few little shouts, like yelps of pain. There were creatures everywhere, sitting under rocks and hugging their knees, lying on their backs and staring up, wandering to and fro, aimlessly, clawing at their skin and their hair and shaking their heads. Some were talking to themselves. Others wrung their hands or pounded the air. Here and there, a figure reared up, beating its chest and bellowing with rage, or screeched and tore at the ground.

They came to the edge of a great black lake. It looked like a liquid swamp in which countless things have rotted over countless centuries. A Wepsoll clung to a withered shrub and rubbed its head against a branch. A Zephor slouched by, mumbling to itself. A Xanthis pointed up at the sky and guffawed, vilely.

But there was another creature, too. It was sitting by the lake, hunched mournfully on a rock. They went towards it. It started to turn.

It had long, thin limbs, pinched shoulders, a long, thin, worn-looking face with a large hook nose, and horny claws with long, drooping talons. Its skin was strange: all faded and dry, and there were just a few wisps of thin grey hair on its head. But it was the eyes that Jemima noticed most. They were very dark and very melancholy, and they seemed to be looking at something very far away.

Slowly, Delphine approached the creature. It stared silently over her shoulder and into the distance.

'I don't suppose you believe in friends,' said Delphine, at last.

'Friends?' said the creature.

'You'll be able to find friends, here.'

'Ahah,' said the creature, disbelievingly. Then it glared. 'You're not part of any empire, are you?' it said. Delphine shook her head, and the creature fell silent again. Jemima tiptoed a little closer. The creature's head swung scrawnily round. Jemima took three steps backward, very quickly, and almost fell over.

'Unaccustomed,' muttered the creature, after a while. 'To . . . *friends*, that is. I possessed no friends, you see. Not ever. In the beginning, it was not of the slightest consequence,' and it stared away into the distance again.

'Why don't you tell us your story?' said Delphine, encouragingly.

'Shall I?' said the creature, turning to Jemima.

'I wish you would,' said Jemima, nodding her head.

'It is short,' said the creature, 'and easily told.'

'We shall be all the more enthralled,' said Grandma, and she settled herself on a rock, and looked very expectant.

'I lived,' said the creature, 'on a planet of my own. A very modest planet, I assure you. But it was mine and no one else's, and I loved it very much. I lived there for a very long time, minding my business, my volcanoes and my tree.'

'I beg your pardon?' said Jemima.

'Two volcanoes,' the creature explained, 'and a single tree. One hardly needs more, on a small planet like mine. I cleaned my volcanoes out regularly. I watered my tree and pruned it. And my planet had its own little sun, so I watched the sun go up and the sun go down, which it did rather often, and I was happy. I could have been happy for ever,' it said.

'So why weren't you?' said Grandma.

'The Steldecks came,' said the creature, simply. Jemima, Grandma and Delphine all frowned. 'A shipful of them. They wanted my planet. I don't know why. There wasn't room for them all. Hardly enough for half a dozen, in fact. They wanted my sun and my volcanoes. They even wanted my tree,' and the creature looked very mournful. Jemima clenched her teeth and gave a soundless growl, the way children sometimes can. 'They told me to go,' said the creature, 'so I left.'

'How?' said Jemima.

'Silently,' said the creature.

'I mean, how did you manage to fly?'

'Easily,' said the creature.

'But you'd never flown before, had you?'

'All the more reason,' said the creature, 'to fly proficiently, when I was finally obliged to. Now, you would think, would you not, that to have one's own planet was a great good fortune?'

'Yes.'

'That to lose it would be a misfortune equally great?'

'Of course.'

'Impossible, you would suppose, that greater fortune or more drastic misfortune could lie in wait for any creature?'

'Impossible.'

'You would be wrong,' said the creature, with great finality. 'I journeyed through the Universe for many years,' it went on. 'I found nothing of any beauty. Nothing, that is, that could compare with my planet. I encountered only *disheartening* things. I *grew* disheartened. And then . . . I saw it.'

'What?'

'The Comet of Comets,' the creature whispered.

Delphine leant forward. *'Really?'* she said. The creature nodded.

'What are you talking about?' said Jemima, turning to Delphine.

'The Comet of Comets,' said Delphine, breathlessly. 'It's supposed to be one of the great splendours of the Universe. There are many legends about it, but almost no one has ever seen it. What was it like?' she asked the creature.

'A miracle,' said the creature, very softly. 'I came upon it quite by chance one day, in a remote corner of the Universe. It kept to the remotest corners, you know. It was wandering along, very slowly, changing colour as it went: brilliant silver, amber, gold; azure and emerald green; cobalt blue and the purest white. It shimmered. It never stopped shimmering. It seemed almost transparent. As though it were the ghost of something else. And there was a sound, too. Musical. Very faint, like the tinkle of tiny bells.' The creature paused.

'Was,' said Delphine, at last.

A look of great grief crossed the creature's face. 'I followed it for year after year,' it said. 'I loved it, the way I had loved my planet. But one day some Earthers found it, and they blew it to bits.'

'I don't know what they were doing there,' said the creature, dully, after a while. 'Earthers don't usually get to the remotest corners at all. But they blew the comet to pieces, and then they took the pieces away. Souvenirs that they could sell, they said,' and the creature grimaced, and looked very disgusted. Then it gazed out steadily across the black lake. Jemima, Grandma and Delphine all gazed, too. 'So there really wasn't anything else to do,' said the creature, after a while. 'I was told about here. I set out. Now I have arrived,' and with those words it lowered its head to its breast and sat there, absolutely still.

'Is there anything we can give you?' said Delphine. The creature appeared not to hear. 'I'd like to help, if I can,' she said, more loudly. There was silence.

Jemima took a step forwards, swayed uncertainly on her feet, then halted, awkwardly. She started to stretch a hand out towards the creature, and then stopped. Somehow, it seemed quite beyond her reach. She looked at Delphine and Delphine looked at her. Then, slowly, they turned again, and, with Grandma behind them, tramped away from the lake, and back up the steep sides of the hollow. There really wasn't anything else to do.

Ten

'So the Archons failed.'

'Yes, Commander. They failed.'

Unit 9 of Earth Spacefleet had arrived at the edge of the Zone. Chief Commander DK was sitting opposite Jemima's father in the control room of the *Andromeda*. He looked handsome and cool.

'Your account of events, if you please,' said the Chief Commander.

'It was unbelievable, Sir. The rays entered the . . . RRR 6427. And then they stopped.' Jemima's father shook his head, and stared at the floor. 'I mean, it was as if they were hitting some sort of wall.' His voice grew loud. 'They just vanished, like streams in sand.'

'I beg your pardon?'

'The rays. They just disappeared.'

'That is not exactly what you said.'

'Like streams, Sir,' said Jemima's father, uncomfortably. 'You know. The way they peter out in sandy ground.'

'*Peter out*?'

'Yes.'

DK looked mildly baffled.

'But RRR 6427 is not any kind of ground.'

'I know, Sir.'

'Rays are rays. Streams are streams. Streams are composed of water.'

'Yes, Sir.'

'In Earth Spacefleet, we speak of walls, streams and sand only when those are the things we mean.'

Jemima's father was silent.

'Are you unwell, QX?'

'No, Sir.'

'Have you become aware of alterations in your moods or bodily functions since you arrived here?'

'No, Sir. You see, our daughter . . .'

'Some very curious events are taking place in this section of the Universe. It is possible that a hostile presence has invaded RRR 6427. This presence may be protecting itself partly by spreading new forms of disease.' DK looked searchingly at Jemima's father. 'RRR 6427 is of crucial importance to us. No one must deprive us of it. All staff should therefore be alert at all times.' He looked at Jemima's father again, warily, as though he were an alien being. 'You and QY will surrender command of the *Andromeda* at once, and report to the doctor.'

'Please, Sir . . .'

'I would prefer not to have to summon the guards to escort you there.'

All of a sudden, Jemima's father gave out a long, despairing groan.

'You see what I mean?' said the Commander, softly. 'You are clearly not yourself.'

*

'*Doleful*. That's *my* word for it. It was an utterly doleful sight.'

Jemima woke up. It was Grandma's voice.

'Is there *nothing* you can offer them by way of a cure?'

A sharp little pain started pinching inside Jemima's head. She was frightened of opening her eyes – but she did, all the same.

She was back in the peach-coloured building again. It was the same little courtyard as before. She was lying on a couch, with Grandma and Delphine sitting nearby.

'Sometimes, yes,' said Delphine, quietly. 'But I'm afraid many of them will never be cured.'

The sun was setting, and the sky was turning from orange to brown as they watched. A breeze flapped lightly at Jemima's curls. She sobbed, loudly, just once. It sounded a bit like a hiccup. Then she got up, went and sat down beside Delphine, and leant against her shoulder. Delphine put her arm around her and hugged her. Then they sat there and watched the sky grow dark.

'You see,' said Delphine, 'for some creatures . . . it's as though another creature had taken you over. Imagine a little monster, creeping up on you in the night. To start with, you don't even know it's there. But it fastens itself to you and clings. Then you realize. You struggle. You try to shake it off, but you can't. The monster just tightens its hold. And then you know that it's going to be there for good.'

Jemima shuddered. 'It's like one of my nightmares,' she said.

'So I can't help the Others very much, you see,' said Delphine. 'But they need me, all the same.'

Then Jemima cried for rather a long time after all, and Delphine held her, and Grandma fussed and clucked.

'Well,' said Grandma, at last, 'and the moral of *this* story is that you can't take little spaceships into great lost zones without . . .'

Delphine looked at her, warningly, and raised a hand.

There were bangings coming from outside, screechings and shouts. The noise was getting nearer, too.

A few moments later, and the courtyard was full of Space Pirates, with Claw and Hood in the middle of them. The bald one and the one with goggles were clutching two little prisoners: Ichamar and Yetta.

'THIS,' roared Claw, 'IS POSITIVELY OUR LAST WORD! LET US OUT ! OR . . .'

But Delphine just shook her head.

'Er . . . you don't seem to understand,' said Claw. 'We have captured your palace. You have no choice but to surrender. Have you?' he added, in a slightly appealing tone of voice.

'Yes we have,' said Delphine.

'Oh dear,' said Claw, looking rather muddled. 'You're not going to complicate matters again, are you?'

'You've captured a courtyard,' said Delphine, 'that's all.'

'The whole palace,' said Claw, obstinately. 'The hub and heartland – as it were – of this little world of yours.'

'Very well,' said Delphine, laughingly. 'Then we'll have to freeze you solid again.'

'Curses,' said Claw. 'I was blindly convinced that we were about to succeed at last. Forgive me. One moment.' He clutched his beard and twisted his claw and muttered to himself for a while.

'I appear to have forgotten something,' he said, at last.

'Hostages,' said Hood, slowly.

'I beg your pardon?'

'Hostages.'

'But of course,' said Claw. 'Apologies to all.' He drew himself up straight again, and squared his shoulders. 'We can scarcely bear with this, can we?' he roared.

'Nossir,' said Hood.

'Our liberty is an imperative, is it not?'

'Yessir.'

'We must resort to menaces, is that not so?'

'Yessir.'

'Very well then. Pay attention!' Claw bellowed to

Delphine. 'As I have said, you have no alternative but to surrender. If you refuse to set us free, we are going to . . . um . . . do some awful things.' He hesitated, then braced himself. 'To our hostages, that is. You do not wish to see them hurt, do you?'

'No,' said Delphine.

Claw looked very relieved.

'But I don't think you'll hurt them anyway,' said Delphine.

'Er . . . you don't?' mumbled Claw.

'No.'

Claw looked at Hood. 'This promises to be disastrous,' he said. He squared his shoulders again. 'We will inflict the most dire torments on our captives!' he roared. Ichamar let out a frightened little yelp.

'What torments, exactly?' said Delphine.

Claw turned in desperation to Hood. But Hood was staring into space. So were all the other pirates. Claw looked at his feet.

'Pinch them,' he muttered. '*Very hard*,' he added, more fiercely.

Delphine laughed.

All of a sudden, Claw stalked wildly over to Ichamar and Yetta and glared at them, very threateningly. He raised his claw. Then he turned back to Delphine; gazed at his claw for a little while; then lowered it to his side.

'Poor Claw,' said Grandma. 'I don't know how he ever got to be a pirate at all. Personally speaking, I'd have rather liked to see him torment that awful little Yetta.'

'Defeat again, Hood,' said Claw.

'Yessir,' said Hood.

'A sad misfortune, is it not?'

'Yessir.'

'We are to remain in thrall to this woman.'
'Yessir.'
'It is we yet again who must throw in the towel. Is that not the case?'
There was a pause. Then,
'Yessir,' said Hood, at last.

*

Ichamar was terribly pleased to be free. He abused the pirates roundly, in sentences that no one could understand. Yetta didn't seem to care so much, and promptly started a rather flirtatious conversation with the pirate in goggles.
'Flibbertigibbet,' said Grandma, with a sniff.
Jemima gazed sympathetically at Claw and Hood. They looked very downcast indeed. She edged towards them, wanting to say something kind, but they were too deep in gloom to notice her. Then Delphine suggested they all eat together, and Jemima made sure she got the seat next to Claw. After a while,
'Mister Claw,' she said, timidly.
'Either *Captain*,' said the pirate, gruffly, 'or just plain Claw.'
'When I grow up,' said Jemima, 'I'd like to be a Space Pirate.'
'Hmmmmph,' said Claw.
'What's it like?' asked Jemima.
All of a sudden, Claw cheered up again. 'EXHILARATING!' he boomed. 'The best life of all. The *only* life. One wanders as one pleases, you see. Rambles through the galaxies. Stops off at any star or planet that takes one's fancy.'
'I'd like that,' said Jemima.
'And then there are the sights,' said Claw. 'Huge red suns. INCALCULABLY vast. Intergalactic storms,

endless clouds of dust . . . they're the ruins of lost worlds, you know. As for the creatures . . .'

'What creatures?' asked Jemima.

'Creatures,' said Claw, 'of every imaginable kind. One never knows what one might see next. Creatures that stand on their heads and shriek. Creatures that die one moment and are reborn the next. Creatures that lost themselves in dreams, an eternity ago, and never woke up again.'

'How very exciting,' said Jemima.

'Above all,' said Claw, 'Space Pirates have adventures.'

'Tell me about them too,' said Jemima.

'Many's the time,' said Claw, grandly, 'that my life has been saved by the merest chance. Or by Hood.'

'By *Hood*?' said Jemima.

Claw nodded. 'He looks good for very little, I freely admit. But in matters of life and death, Hood is indispensable.'

Jemima gazed at Hood with new respect. Hood was staring into space, as usual.

'And then there are the raids,' said Claw.

'Ahah,' said Jemima, conspiratorially. Claw looked just a little embarrassed.

'Hardly worth a mention, really,' he said. 'Trifling affairs, I assure you. We only attack the very smallest ships.'

'Isn't that a bit like bullying?'

'It's only the small ones we can beat,' said Claw, apologetically.

'Just as I thought,' said Jemima. 'You're bullies.'

'Oh dear,' said Claw, clutching his head. 'We only pick on the villains, you know.'

'But pirates *are* villains,' said Jemima.

'By no means,' said Claw, in a horrified tone.

'Yes they are,' said Jemima. 'Pirates are always villains. Everybody knows that.'

'The vilest of slanders!' boomed Claw. 'It is Earthers, Archons and Steldecks who are the villains!'

'But I'm an Earther,' said Jemima.

'I shall consider you an honourable exception,' said Claw.

'I suppose that's what you think you are, too.'

'Precisely. As the Universe wags, pirates must indeed be thought of as honourable exceptions. To enlarge on my point, I shall tell you a story.'

'Oh good,' said Jemima, clapping her hands, and she settled down to listen.

Eleven

'The story in question,' said Claw, 'was told to me by a fellow pirate named Rufus. It is true in all particulars.'

'How do you know?' asked Jemima.

'Pirate captains never lie,' said Claw, 'at least, not when telling stories. It is part of their code of honour, you know. Now on this occasion, Rufus had travelled a very great distance. Far beyond the traders and the warships; further than the furthest satellite. He had passed beyond the borders of the Empires, and headed out towards the remotest regions of all, where the very strangest worlds are to be found. It was one of those worlds that he reached.'

Claw paused.

'It was a world of creatures who were *both everything and nothing*.'

'I beg your pardon?' said Grandma. Claw was telling his story very well. Everyone else had started to listen, too.

'In themselves they were nothing. They were everything else, instead.'

'Everything and nothing,' said Grandma.

Claw nodded.

'I see,' said Grandma, in a strangled sort of way. 'One of those again,' and she groaned.

'I do not mean to suggest,' said Claw, 'that they were all things at one moment. Merely that they were capable of becoming everything, given time.'

'So what did they look like?' said Grandma.

'They resembled whatever they became, of course. They might start out – as an Archon, let us say. Very well then. An Archon would take shape before one's eyes, growing more substantial from second to second, more and more like an Archon, with more and more Archon features . . .'

'How very repellent,' said Grandma, shuddering. 'And then?'

'Nothing,' said Claw.

'*Nothing*?'

'A puff of smoke. A tiny gust of wind. Then nothing, save a few little threads of mist.'

'A fate,' said Grandma, 'that one might heartily wish on all Archons.'

'And then a different creature would begin to appear.'

'Like a ghost,' said Jemima. 'I mean, they really were like ghosts, weren't they. What Earthers used to call ghosts, that is.'

'The ghosts *I* recall . . .' said Grandma – Jemima

coughed incredulously – '. . . were ghosts of the living. Now as I understand it, there was never anything there in the first place for these creatures to be ghosts of.'

'But perhaps they felt a little like ghosts,' said Claw.

'Yes,' said Jemima, 'never quite real. I expect they were dreadfully unhappy,' and she sighed.

'Not in the least,' said Claw, firmly.

'I certainly would be,' said Grandma.

'But their lives were of great interest to them, you see,' said Claw. 'They knew so much . . . from *inside*, as it were.'

'All the same,' said Grandma, 'I would rather be Jemima's Grandma, and nothing else, than everything else, and not Jemima's grandma.'

'But of course,' said Claw, and he flourished his claw, solemnly, and bowed in Jemima's direction, 'if Jemima were one's grandchild. Nevertheless: to think the thoughts, to feel the feelings of so very many beings . . .'

'. . . would be enormously confusing,' Grandma put in.

'Rufus said it made them very tired,' said Claw, 'but also gentle and kind.'

'But why an honourable exception?' said Jemima, suddenly.

'I beg your pardon?' said Claw.

'Pirates are honourable exceptions, you said. That's what the story was supposed to show.'

'Simple,' said Claw. 'You see, Rufus never *told* anyone.'

There was a silence.

'Anyone, that is, but other pirates. And pirates do not pass on stories that have been told to them in confidence. Not to anyone they do not trust.'

'I'm afraid the point escapes me,' said Grandma. 'Rufus left the planet. Good. Rufus never mentioned it. Good. I fail to see why this should make him an honourable . . .'

'The zoos,' said Claw, darkly.

'Ah,' said Grandma, and she shut her mouth with a very loud clack.

'Earthers love zoos,' said Claw, 'but they aren't the only ones. The Archons love the Space Zoos just as much as the Earthers, and so do the Steldecks. They fill them with strange creatures, and then gawp at them.'

Jemima nodded, hard.

'But Rufus was very fond of the creatures he'd discovered. He thought they were quite the wisest creatures he'd ever known, and he didn't want them to be gawped at.'

'Bravo, Rufus!' said Grandma, stoutly.

'He cried a little when he left,' said Claw. 'He knew he'd never go back, you see. He even tore up his spacemap.'

'So no one's going to find them again,' said Jemima.

'Let us hope not, at any rate,' said Grandma.

Someone approached the table and whispered to Delphine. Everybody waited. Delphine glanced round.

'To be sold to the Earthers or the Archons would be bad enough,' she said quietly. 'But the Steldecks . . . The Steldecks are the worst of all. The cleverest, the cruellest, the most malevolent. Don't you think so, Claw?'

Claw did.

'Well,' said Delphine, 'they've arrived,' and she frowned. 'There are Steldeck ships at the edge of the Zone.'

Twelve

Before very long, the Steldecks had started to *summon*. They'd summoned Zendis for a meeting. They'd summoned DK, too. He was on his way there now, in a spaceboat, with ten of his crew. They were making their way towards a great black metal wall. Steldeck ships were always black.

'It's their Command Headquarters,' said DK. 'I shall be meeting their most important chiefs, I expect.'

A yellow square appeared in the dark, and the pilot steered towards it. They flew into a gigantic yellow hall; and then touched down.

In a moment, the spaceship was surrounded.

There were Steldecks on all sides. Fearsome. Huge. Three times as tall as anyone from Earth. They stood upright on two long legs, and had heads that turned, swivelling, like scanners; oval heads, like eggs on their sides, with single red eyes where the tops should have been. Their bodies were hard-shelled, creamy in colour, and looked sickly and repulsive. They craned above the Earthers, shifting back and forth. Each of the Steldecks had a weapon. Each of the weapons was pointing down.

'Disembark,' whispered DK. 'Politely, if you can.'

The crew did their best to disembark politely. The Steldecks waited and watched. Then one of them slowly screwed its head round and nodded. It was pointing in the direction of a door. The Earthers went through.

Then the Steldecks led them down a passage, and then another, and another. The yellow light got brighter and hurt their eyes. A buzzing noise dinned in their ears. That was the machines. There were machines . . . well, everywhere. Super-computers, monster robots – nothing on Earth was at all that big. Some of them watched you and recorded everything you did. Others noted the pace of your breath or the sound of your step. They monitored your heartbeat. They measured the power of your brain. They forecast your future and pondered your past. They tracked you down in your smallest cells, and flashed the facts on a thousand screens.

It was a dizzying walk; exhausting, too. When it came to an end, DK realized he was in the control room.

So were Zendis and the Archons. So were the Steldeck chiefs. Chillith, Gerin, Prandahl . . .

But there was something else to look at, too. In the

middle of the control room was a tall metal tower, and on top of the tower was . . . a small black bomb. It had a funny, pointed head, and round, hard, glittering eyes.

'Its name is Magda, DK.' It was Chillith who spoke. 'It is the most powerful computer in the Universe.'

DK and the bomb surveyed each other. 'Welcome,' said Magda, in a humming whine.

'We have brought it here,' said Chillith, 'to discover what has happened in RRR 6427, and to . . . resolve our problem.'

'Resolved already,' said Magda, promptly. 'Problem resolved in its entirety. With replications. *Ad infinitum.*'

'No doubt, Magda,' said Chillith. 'We have the highest faith in your powers.'

'Justly,' said Magda.

'Nonetheless,' said Chillith, 'there are some final data for you to absorb.' He turned to DK. 'Where are the commanders of the *Andromeda*?'

'They . . .'

'They are not here,' Magda interrupted.

'Why?'

'They . . .'

'They are ill,' said Magda, again.

'Of what?'

DK stared pointedly at Magda. 'Perhaps you'd like to tell me,' he said.

'Corruption of the brain cells,' said Magda, at once. 'Specific. Contingent. Non-endemic. And now I must ask *you*: did you lose a craft?'

'Yes.'

'Were persons of importance lost with it?'

'No.'

'Then shortly afterwards,' said Chillith, 'if I am not mistaken, the Archons arrived, and attempted to destroy RRR 6427.'

'That is correct,' said Zendis, coming forwards.

'Why did you not succeed?'

'We do not know. We fired rays of huge power. They simply did not reach their target.'

All of a sudden, Magda began to whirr, very rapidly, and very loudly. Then it emitted a loud screeching noise; clicked, clicked, clicked and clicked again. Then it went quiet.

'Information complete,' it said. 'Situation comprehended. In – I must stress – every possible ramification. Solution devised and available now.'

'What is your solution?' said Chillith.

'9882517,' said Magda. 'Planet CYTW. The problem is the same. The solution, too. I will be instrumental.'

'I understand,' said Chillith.

'Then kindly translate for the rest of us,' said DK.

'From time to time,' said Chillith, 'you Earthers have rebellions in your Empire, do you not?'

DK agreed. They did.

'So, too, with the Archons,' said Chillith. 'Even we have them, on occasions.' His one eye blinked. 'It is usually very easy for us to suppress these rebellions.

The rebels are weak, and we are immensely strong. But with Planet CYTW this was not the case.'
'They managed to resist you?' said DK.
'For a very long time,' said Chillith. 'You see, they had found a way of fighting us with their *minds*. They used them to hold us at bay, to bring our ships down, in many other ways, too. We couldn't defeat them.'
'But presumably you did in the end,' said DK.
'Of course,' said Chillith. 'We were completing our work on Magda at that time. When we had finished it, we instructed Magda to defeat the rebels. And Magda did.'
'I shall also defeat these rebels,' said Magda. 'Their cells do have a quite peculiar vigour. But it is by no means equal to mine.'
Zendis turned on his heel, and walked to the door.
'Where are you going?' said Chillith. Zendis stared.
'To prepare our guns. You neutralize the enemy. We destroy RRR 6427.'
'*Destroy* it?'
'Why not?'
'You Archons can be very foolish,' said Chillith, slowly. 'Why do you suppose the Earthers got here first?'
Zendis shrugged.
'*Wealth*,' said Chillith. 'Riches and resources beyond compare. Is that not the case, DK?'
DK stared ahead of him, and said nothing.
'But we have the stronger fleet,' said Chillith. 'When Magda has done its work, we Steldecks will be the first to explore RRR 6427. You Archons may follow us. The Earthers should perhaps come last. What do you think, Zendis?'
Zendis glared at DK. It was a long, slow, ferocious

glare. Then he nodded. Chillith turned to the tower.

'Begin, Magda,' he said. 'Eradicate the enemy. And let us hope that the Empires suffer no more disruptions, of this or any other kind.'

*

'They're not doing anything,' said Jemima to Grandma. 'I mean, maybe they're not going to attack at all.'

They were back at Fitzmaranda's, staring at the screen.

'Oh, they'll attack,' said Delphine, 'and they'll be very hard to beat, too. We'll need to use all our strength.'

'Are you going to use our minds this time?' said Jemima, hopefully.

Delphine shook her head.

'You may use *our* minds, if you wish,' said Claw. 'I flatter myself that they might be of some service.'

Delphine shook her head again. Vigorously. Claw frowned.

'You clearly underestimate the pirate intellect,' he muttered.

Lots of different creatures were coming crowding into the room. Delphine hurried about, talking to them all. Jemima crept over to Claw.

'Don't be upset, Mister Claw,' she said.

'Plain Claw to you, Jemima,' said Claw. 'I really must insist. As with my peers in piracy.'

'But I'm not a pirate,' said Jemima.

'In deed, no,' said Claw, 'but in spirit . . . well . . .'

Jemima looked at him, and grinned.

The enemy ships were all very still. No firing this time. But the creatures in the room had fallen silent again. Jemima, Grandma and the pirates huddled together and watched.

Suddenly, Delphine and the others staggered. It was just as if they'd all been punched, very hard; as if a spacequake had shaken the room. No one fell. But it took them a moment to stand up straight again. Claw looked anxious.

'What was that?' he asked.

'We're under attack,' said Grandma, breezily. 'But we'll win in the end. We always do.'

Jemima looked about her. The trouble was . . . she wasn't quite sure that Grandma was right. All the creatures were still on their feet. But their shoulders were starting to droop and their tummies were sticking out. They looked very tired – sometimes even in pain.

Then they started to groan. Their heads bowed, and their knees bent. Jemima and the others stared, appalled.

And then the faces relaxed again. The knees straightened, and the heads went up.

'Just as I claimed,' said Grandma, and she folded her arms and looked very superior. 'We are simply invincible.'

Delphine was standing upright. Her eyes were opening.

'It seems to me,' said Grandma, 'that the habit of victory . . .'

Delphine swayed on her feet; then stumbled, and almost fell. Claw caught her, just in time.

Jemima looked round, aghast. Some of the creatures were lying on the ground. Others were clinging to the walls. Others were holding their heads, or kneeling, bent over, with their faces to the floor.

'Is the pain very bad?' said Claw, gently.

'They have . . . some source of terrible power with them,' said Delphine. 'I'm very afraid it's stronger than we are.'

'But you've defeated it!' shouted Grandma.

Delphine shook her head. 'It has simply run out of energy for a while,' she said. 'But it will start again, very soon.'

'So we must watch it all a second time?' said Claw, shivering. Delphine smiled, wearily. 'It is not a pleasant spectacle,' said Claw, after a while.

'But you can go now.'

'I beg your pardon?' said Claw.

'You are free to leave us, on two conditions.'

'The first?'

'You take the little girl too, and the old lady.'

'And the second?' said Claw, grimly.

'You must turn us into one of your pirate stories. Then you must tell it as often as you can.'

Claw looked at Hood. 'Hood,' he said, at last, 'we have permission to go.'

'Yessir.'

'We can resume our pirating ways.'

'Yessir.'

'This is what we have wanted, Hood. This is what we have been waiting for.'

'Yessir.'

'Nonetheless, Hood . . .'

'Yessir?'

'It seems to me that to desert our friends in their hour of need would be the act of scoundrels. Do you not think so?'

'Yessir,' said Hood, at last. Claw turned to Jemima.

'You see?' he said. 'Just as I told you. In certain predicaments, the man is indispensable.'

Delphine was standing again, now, and signalling to the others.

'They'll attack again soon,' she said. Then she smiled. 'Maybe they're weaker now, like us.'

But they weren't.

*

The second attack was very much worse than the first. Delphine and the others went spinning to the walls. The invisible force bent their bodies, twisted them, flung them round and made them moan with pain. It knocked them off their feet and threw them to the floor. When the battle stopped again, they were lying there, helpless and still.

Claw went over to Delphine and cradled her in his arms. He chattered to her, lightly, as though she were a child. He even tried to sing to her, in a funny voice, that was sometimes shrill and sometimes gruff. At last, Delphine opened her eyes.

'I had a question for you,' she said to Claw, and she gripped his wrist. 'Rufus. Is he still alive?' Claw nodded, silently. 'I'm glad,' said Delphine. 'He still remembers those creatures, doesn't he?'

'He never forgets them,' said Claw. 'He says they haunt his dreams.' Delphine squeezed Claw's arm.

'This time,' she said, 'you really must go.'

Thirteen

Chief Commander DK had gone back to his fleet. He was standing in his control room, now, and staring at a screen. The dots on the screen were bubbling wildly. Then Chillith's head appeared.

'DK?'

'Receiving you.'

'I am pleased to be able to inform you,' said Chillith, 'that Magda has virtually crushed the enemy. It is pausing for a moment to boost its power, and it will then complete the operation.'

'And after that?' said DK. 'We will follow your instructions, of course,' he added, in a surly tone.

'We enter RRR 6427, together. We proceed to destroy what remains of the enemy and its habitations. We then explore RRR 6427. In turn.'

'Very good,' said DK.

'You do not look very pleased, DK. You should. Yet again it has proved impossible to defy the Empires with impunity. Our sway is supreme throughout the Universe. Long may it continue so,' and, with those words, Chillith inclined his head a little, and then disappeared from the screen. DK turned to one of his crew.

'Ships to be ready for entry into RRR 6427. For battle, too. *Andromeda* to remain outside, with QX, QY and a crew of twelve on board.'

The crewman turned to go.

'All ships are to be *fully prepared* for battle. You understand, Officer?'

'Yes, Commander.'

'To *remain* fully prepared for battle, even after the enemy has been annihilated.' And Commander DK let out a low, wily chuckle, and began to punch fiercely at a set of controls.

*

Back at Fitzmaranda's, Jemima was gazing at the Steldeck ships. They were hanging there, just waiting, like greedy fat-bellied insects. It was unbearable, it was, oh . . . she brandished her fists. Then she ran shrieking at the screen. It was Claw who caught her. He ran after her, grabbed her, then hugged her, very hard. Slowly, Jemima quietened down.

'We must go,' said Claw, softly, at last.

'But I can't just leave them!' shouted Jemima.

Delphine was on her feet again, now. 'Listen, Jemima,' she said. 'Very soon, there will be nothing left of the Great Lost Zone, except for one tiny little bit, and that's the bit that's there in you. You must take it away with you. Out into the Universe.'

'NO!' yelled Jemima, and she tore herself free of Claw's grip and hurled herself in a passion at the screen. Then three figures appeared.

It was Fitzmaranda, Clyst and Cheng. They looked exhausted and ill. But their eyes were excited and alive.

'Tell them, Clyst,' said Fitzmaranda. Clyst stepped forwards, threw his head back, and gazed at Delphine.

'You will remember,' he said, 'that I had made contact with creatures from another universe.'

Delphine nodded, expectantly.

'I am now in regular contact with them,' said Clyst.

'Clyst,' said Delphine, 'you are . . .'

'Prodigious,' said Clyst. 'I readily admit it. Their universe is called Vidanda. It is mysterious. Marvellous. Quite beyond our comprehension. We shall be safe there.'

'Safe?' said Delphine. 'What do you mean?'

'I mean,' said Clyst, 'that the Vidandans and I have found a way of transporting the whole of the Zone to Vidanda.' Everyone stared at him in amazement. 'Yes,' said Clyst, '*the whole of the Zone*. The Vidandans will help us, if we can join our power with theirs.'

'And we can,' said a voice.

It was Cheng who had spoken, in a tiny, beautiful, musical voice. It seemed somehow to come from very far away.

'We still have the strength,' she said.

'But the Steldecks must think we have been defeated,' said Fitzmaranda. 'We must appear to surrender. It will help us conserve our energies. Then,

as the Steldecks approach the Zone, we launch it . . .'
'Into Vidanda!' shouted Clyst.
The idea left everyone speechless for a while. Then, 'What will happen to them?' said Delphine. 'The Steldecks and the rest?'
'ANNIHILATED!' bellowed Grandma, in glee. Then she clapped her hand across her mouth. 'Oh dear,' she said, 'I quite forgot myself.' But Clyst shook his head.
'The hole the Zone leaves will suck them in and then cast them out again. They will be scattered across the Universe,' and he clicked his fingers sharply, with some satisfaction.
Jemima jumped up and down with delight. 'Vidanda!' she crowed. 'What fun!'
Everyone looked at her, uncomfortably. Then Delphine took her hand. 'No, Jemima,' she said. 'Not you.' Jemima stared at her in disbelief.
'What about your parents?' said Delphine. 'They'd lose you for ever.'
'My *parents*?' said Jemima. 'They won't even notice I've gone.'
'I'm afraid I'm not so sure,' said Grandma, all at once.
'In any case,' said Delphine, 'I've told you before: you don't have our strength. You wouldn't survive.'
Jemima sat down hard on the floor.
'And us?' said Claw, nervously. 'We have no wish to be . . . scattered, I think, was the word.'
'We'll propel you out of the Zone as we leave,' said Fitzmaranda.
'Free at last, then, Hood,' said Claw.
'Yessir,' said Hood.
'Free, and at our ease. And *proud*.'
All of a sudden, Hood gulped.
'Permission to speak,' he said.

'To speak?' said Claw, startled.

'Yes.'

'This is rather irregular, Hood.'

'Yes,' said Hood, staring at him.

'You are not in the habit of speaking when not spoken to.'

'I'm changing 'em,' said Hood. 'My habits, that is.'

'*Exceedingly* irregular,' said Claw, with a sigh, 'but I suppose I had better hear you.'

'When we're free . . .' Hood took a deep breath.

'Yes?' said Claw.

'I want a turn at being captain,' said Hood. 'Please,' he added, after a moment's thought.

'*Captain*?' said Claw.

'Yes.'

'To be captain,' said Claw, 'is my task, Hood.'

'I want my turn,' said Hood, doggedly.

Claw coughed. 'Some men,' he said, 'are marked out for captaincy. It simply follows, as the night the day. I am one of those men. You – alas – fall somewhat short. Such is the way of things. Sorry, old fellow, but there it is.'

'You mean you're not going to let me,' said Hood, darkly.

'A question of destiny, rather,' said Claw.

'Then there's going to be a *mutiny*,' said Hood. 'You mark my words,' and he shut his mouth, abruptly, and went back to staring into space.

All of a sudden, Jemima leapt up from the floor, ran over to Delphine, and grabbed her by the arm.

'I'll never see you again, will I,' she said, tearfully.

Delphine patted her head. 'Jemima,' she said, 'even creatures like the Steldecks can't stay the way they are for ever. Some day, everything will be different, and then we'll return . . .'

'As pirates, perhaps,' said Claw.

Delphine laughed. Then she quivered.

'They're starting again,' she said. Fitzmaranda came up.

'Everyone has been informed of our plan,' he said. 'Clyst and Cheng will shortly make contact with the Vidandans.'

The control room fell silent. Before very long, the invisible force was at work again, wrenching bodies out of shape and bending them to the floor. The room shuddered, very violently, as though a vast bird had banged it with its wing. The walls started snapping and cracking, splintering, splitting apart. Then everything began to shake . . .

And then the noises seemed to fade away. The room was shuddering, frantically. But it also felt peaceful and still. Everything went white – a flickering, luminous, phantom white. Clyst, Delphine, Fitzmaranda, Cheng – they were turning into ghosts.

'Let's go!' bellowed Claw. He hustled Jemima to the door, with Hood and Grandma right behind.

Out in the corridor, Jemima suddenly stopped. 'Oh no,' she said, 'we've lost Birmingham again!'

Claw stared at her, in fright. Then the two of them turned, ran back, and flung the door open.

It was . . . beyond belief.

The room was alight. It was burning with a pure white fire. Delphine and the others had all become single flames. And there, spinning madly in the middle, was an eerie little silver robot.

'Don't!' screamed Jemima. But it was too late. Claw had hurled himself into the fire and disappeared.

But he came back again, too – and he had Birmingham with him.

'I was rude to you once,' said Jemima, 'but I take it back, now. You're not a softie at all.'

Claw held up his one hand in protest. 'My dear little girl,' he said, 'let us merely suppose that I *vary*. Like every other creature in the Universe.'

They looked at each other, and grinned. Then they hurried off. They ran out of the room and stopped for a moment, gasping for breath. The flames were everywhere, now. They scuttled out of the building and away to the pirate ships. They clambered aboard, and Claw went straight to the controls.

Jemima stared at the building, the landscape . . . It was all transparent, now. As though it were somehow just ebbing away. The engines started with a squeal. Then, 'Look!' cried Claw.

There, spreading triumphantly across the sky, the fleets of the Empires came thundering into view. The next moment . . .

It was as if something were pushing them gently upwards through a gigantic gale. The ships from the fleets went spinning away crazily in all directions; and the pirates and their friends went floating slowly, up and out, towards a vast expanse of quiet stars.

Fourteen

After a while, Claw and Jemima looked back again, towards the place where the Zone had been.

'Now it really *is* lost,' said Jemima, sadly. 'For good. And we're the only ones who ever knew.'

Grandma came bustling up. 'Birmingham is on the road to recovery,' she announced. 'He has just *bleeped*.'

They hurried away to have a look. Birmingham was standing in a corner, looking just a little scorched, but otherwise unscathed.

'Birmingham?' said Jemima, anxiously.

There was a long silence. Then a bleep.

'How are you, Birmingham?' said Grandma.

Birmingham bleeped again. Then he bleeped repeatedly. Then he whirred for a while, and emitted a sort of harsh, metallic snarl. And then he started to talk very rapidly in a sharp tinny voice that wasn't like his own voice at all.

'Can you multiply nineteen thousand four hundred and eleven by eight thousand nine hundred and sixty-two?'

Grandma gaped. 'Of course not. You know that. And nor can you.'

'The answer is one hundred and seventy-three million nine hundred and sixty-one thousand three hundred and eighty-two. Which star vanished in Earth year 2379 BC?'

Grandma and Jemima stared at each other.

'Sertus. Are creatures fickle because matter is fissile?'

'Birmingham, I don't even understand . . .'

'Undetermined as yet. In a situation of some extremity, may one not be utterly transformed?'

'Listen, Birmingham . . .'

'The answer is yes. The Universe assumes a different complexion which, to the observer, will be properly inseparable from the perception itself of the capacity to change complexion. What could more poignantly demonstrate the effective inexistence of what we habitually take to be . . .'

'I've had enough of this,' muttered Grandma, and she walked over to Birmingham and smacked him smartly on the top of the head. 'Birmingham!' she said.

There was a pause. Then, 'Yes?' said Birmingham.

'You're malfunctioning. Very badly.'

Another pause.

'Anyone for chess?' said Birmingham, at last.

Jemima and Grandma smiled. 'Later,' said Jemima. 'I promise. I won't forget, either.'

'Very well,' said Birmingham, and he hummed for a little, and then went quiet. Jemima turned back to Claw.

'What now?' she asked.

'Is it not obvious?' said Claw. 'We will resume our pirating life – and you will come with us. You will see the most wonderful sights. Stars that go pop! and simply disappear from the sky, like dreams. Creatures on single legs, with heads that buffet the skies. Creatures who live in icy cocoons that tinkle when they talk. Vast and empty planets with vast and empty seas. The most bizarre . . .'

'I want to go back to Earth,' said Grandma.

'Ah, my sweet old lady . . .'

'Watch your manners, pirate.'
'Dear Grandma . . .'
'I am *not* your Grandma.'
'Very well then. Dear friend . . .'
'That's better.'
'I suggest you develop a spirit of adventure.'
There was a noise of hurry and bustle outside. It was Hood, and some of the other pirates with him. They looked fierce and cross.
'This . . .' said Hood. Then he stopped.
'Proceed,' said Claw, encouragingly.
'Er . . . *this* . . .'
'The suspense,' said Claw, 'is well-nigh insupportable.'
Hood glared at him.
'This,' he said, 'is a *mutiny*.'
The pirates all shook their fists, and cried 'MUTINY!' together.
'I see,' said Claw. 'And what is it to issue in, this mutiny of yours?'
Hood looked rather perplexed. He turned to the other pirates and they whispered for a while. Then, 'WE'RE GOING TO MAKE YOU WALK THE PLANK!' he shouted to Claw.
'I have never heard you shout so loud before, Hood,' said Claw. 'You sound . . . stentorian. Congratulations.'
Hood smiled, bashfully, and looked down at his toes.
'There aren't any planks in spaceships,' said Jemima.
Hood and the others looked rather depressed.
'I could always walk off one of the wing-tips,' said Claw, helpfully.
Hood and the others brightened up again. 'A wing-tip,' said Hood, 'will do nicely.'
Claw looked him in the eye. 'I understand,' he said.

'Well, dear friend,' and he turned to Grandma, 'it seems that I must bid you farewell. As for you, Jemima, may I say that it has been a very great pleasure to make your acquaintance. And you, Hood,' he said, 'well . . . I leave you at the helm.'

Hood looked rather baffled at this. 'The helm?' he said, weakly.

'That, I believe, is what it was formerly called,' said Claw. 'Back in the days of good old no-nonsense pirating, that is. I mean, of course, the steering gear.'

There was a silence.

'I don't know how to work the steering gear,' said Hood.

'How unfortunate,' said Claw. 'Perhaps I could show you,' he said.

'I don't think I'd understand,' said Hood.

'But in that case . . .' said Grandma.

'It means . . .' said Jemima.

'That your mutiny is come to grief,' said Claw. 'Now, should we not put this behind us, Hood, and let bygones be bygones?'

Hood and his cronies were just agreeing to this when another pirate came rushing into the room.

'A ship!' he shouted. 'Coming towards us! Now!'

'MAN THE GUNS!' roared Claw.

The crew looked at the floor, in an embarrassed sort of way.

'We can't,' said Hood, at last.

'I beg your pardon?' said Claw.

'We sold them to the Sputans, remember?'

'Alas,' said Claw, slapping his head. 'So we did. At a paltry price, too, if I recall it aright.'

Hood winced.

'Ten crates of Sputan meat pies,' he mumbled.

Claw nodded.

'I got very tired of Sputan meat pies,' said Hood.

Jemima had run to the window. All of a sudden, 'It's the *Andromeda*!' she shouted, and she whooped with joy. Claw looked inquiringly at Grandma.

'Her parents,' Grandma explained. 'She thought they'd been scattered through the Universe, you see. By and large, I'm glad they have not. But it makes matters the more difficult for you, I'm afraid.'

'Why so?' said Claw.

'They're going to arrest you,' said Grandma, with a grin.

*

In a few minutes, Jemima's parents were standing in the pirate ship, with Joshua and a few of their crew. They looked around them, then stared at Claw.

'We have reason to believe,' said Jemima's father, 'that this ship engages in criminal activities.'

'I deny it,' said Claw.

Jemima's father just stared at him again; at Hood, with his scar and his scarf; at the earring and the goggles.

'You are pirates,' he said.

'QX,' said Jemima's mother, 'it's Jemima.'

'First things first,' said her husband, stiffly, not looking at Jemima.

'But she's safe,' said Jemima's mother, trembling.

'It is a question of the law.'

'But . . .'

'Oh, very well then,' said Jemima's father, testily, and he turned to his daughter. 'Jemima, we are really *most* displeased. You know the rules. At no point in time should any craft, however small . . .'

At which point, Grandma came stomping up. 'Here,' she said, pointing, 'is your daughter. Here,' and she prodded her chest, 'is your mother-in-law. For all you knew, we were quite, quite dead. So greet us pleasantly. Embrace your daughter. Or our pirate friends will cast you from their ship without the slightest ceremony.'

Claw and Hood gave each other a nervous look.

All at once, Jemima's mother ran across the room, took Jemima in her arms, and hugged her.

Jemima's father coughed. Hemmed. Stared at the ceiling. Looked at Claw. Then he stumbled a little, sideways; took a tiny, edging step towards the window; paused; took another step, and another. Everyone waited for a minute or so. At last, Jemima's father reached his daughter, bent down slowly, and awkwardly touched her hair.

'Oh Daddy,' said Jemima, hugging him, 'you really are a *very* silly man.'

'And so . . .?' said Grandma, after a pause.

'We'll all be pirates together.' It was Birmingham who had spoken.

'Birmingham,' said Claw, 'you are sublime. Pirates together. Exactly so. The *Andromeda* must join forces with us.'

Jemima's father straightened up again. 'Spacefleet Command,' he said, 'would hardly approve . . .'

'Spacefleet Command be damned!' said Grandma. 'Spacefleet Command thinks you've been scattered through the Universe with everyone else. Don't you understand? You're *free*!'

'But these men are outlaws,' said Jemima's father, feebly.

'Not really,' said Jemima, quickly. 'Not when you get to know them, that is. Then you find out that they're really honourable exceptions,' and she grinned at Claw. Her parents looked at each other.

'It would be very wicked,' said QX.

Jemima's mother giggled. 'But it might be rather fun,' she said.

QX chuckled, too. 'No one would ever know,' he said.

QY started giggling like mad. 'We'll sail away, for a year and a day . . .'

'You'll see the most wonderful sights!' said Jemima. 'Stars that go pop! and disappear from the sky, like dreams. Vast, empty planets with vast empty seas . . .'

'*Surrender*!' boomed Claw. 'Surrender to the lure of the great uncharted wastes!'

Jemima's father turned to him and beamed. 'We'll go and get ready,' he said.

'Bravo!' shouted Claw. Then he winked. 'Fellow *rogue*,' he added. QX stopped; and then winked back.

'MINIONS!' bellowed Claw. 'PREPARE TO DEPART!'

The pirates hurried off to get to work. Jemima's parents disappeared with their crew.

From down below came a thundering sound. The engines were starting up. Grandma joined Jemima, and they gazed out of the window together.

'Do you think they'll ever come back?' said Jemima, at last.

'Sure to, dear,' said Grandma.

'I feel so sorry for them,' said Jemima, with a sigh.

'Oh, I shouldn't do that,' said Grandma. 'I expect the Vidandans are treating them royally by now. Feasts and fun and I don't know what.'

'I don't think the Others would like that,' said Jemima.

'I can see it's unlikely,' said Grandma. 'But then perhaps we should trust to unlikelihood.'

'I might do,' said Jemima, 'if I knew what you meant.'

'Very simple,' said Grandma. 'Earthers always think they know everything. But my point is that you *never* quite know. Which means that the unexpected is always possible. And who knows what might become of anyone in Vidanda anyway. Including the Others.'

Jemima thought for a while. Then, 'Have I really got a bit of the Zone in me,' she asked, 'the way Delphine said?'

Grandma scrutinized her critically. 'My dear,' she said, 'I'm very much afraid that you have. Let us hope that it is not infectious.'

'And you too?'

'Don't talk nonsense,' said Grandma, and she smiled.

A roar came blasting from the engines. The pirate ship was setting out for deep space.

'You know, Grandma,' said Jemima, 'I don't think I'd want to go to another universe.'

'My goodness no,' said Grandma, firmly. 'Not for the present, at any rate. Far too much to do and to see.'

'But maybe in the future?'

'Ah well. The *future*.' Grandma winked. 'In the end, may not you and I be ripe for another little adventure all of our own?'

They looked at each other, smiled, and hugged each other close. Then a soft little buzzing noise came from the door.

It was Birmingham. He was standing there, watching them, with a chessboard spread on his two metal arms. All the pieces were ready laid out.

Jemima groaned. 'All right, Birmingham,' she said, and she fetched a little table and a chair. Slowly, Birmingham trundled over. Slowly he lowered the board. Then, very slowly and very deliberately, he lifted a pawn, moved it six squares forward, and triumphantly captured Jemima's queen.